I0788412

For Cale, Always.

Other Books by Sarah K. L. Wilson

Dragon School Series
First Flight
Initiate
The Dark Prince
The Ruby Isles
Sworn
Dusk Covenant
First Message
Warring Promises
Prince of Dragons
Dark Night
Bright Hopes
Mark of Loyalty
Dire Quest
Ancient Allies
Pipe of Wings
Dragon Piper
Dust of Death
Troubled War
Starie Night
Ascendant Light
Dragon Chameleon Series
Rogue's Quest
Paths of Deception
City of Ice
Mist of Power
Silver Eyes
World of Legends
Chase the Moon
Shadow Quest

Creeping Darkness
Golem Siege
Memory of Mountains
Color of Victory
Dragon Tide Series
Dragonlet
Dragon Staff
Desperate Flight
Bubbles of Hope
Waves of Destiny
Tides of Change
Keys of Power
Rock Eaters
Underworld
Chosen One
The Unweaving Chronicles Series
Teeth of the Gods
Lightning Strikes Twice
Thunder Rattles High
Bridge of Legends Series
Summernight
Dawnspell
Autumngale
Winterfast
Springhatch
Tangled Fae Series
Fae Hunter
Fae Captive
Fae Nightmare

BOOK ONE

"Look too long at the tangled ones and you will find yourself tangling, too. Grow too angry at the injustices done to you, and you will find yourself becoming unjust. Harden your heart too much against the cruelties done against you and you will soon be cruel. But let yourself bleed, let yourself ache, let yourself be maligned, let yourself shed hot tears of sorrow, and from your pain and sorrow will spring up fresh life."
-Wisdom of the Travelers

Chapter One

Wrath. Writhe. Wraith. Wreath.

My hands twisted the willow branches as my mind recited those words again and again. They were the words that Scouvrel told me we derived from the word "wrae" from which we also got the word Fae.

He'd been right that they were all the same. I'd felt the wrath of the Fae when they drowned me in a barrel of wine and tried to pry me from the cage. I'd felt it in how they nailed my father to a tree.

I'd felt the writhing pain of the Fae in the echoes of their false merriment and terrible bargains.

I'd seen how they were twisted like wreaths when I looked at their world with my true sight.

I'd seen how they faded like wraiths of what they could be – like my sister Hulanna who was not human anymore.

Twisted. That's what our ancestors had meant by those words. Twisted by anger, twisted by pain, twisted by death and twisted by hands. They were all twisted.

And I was becoming twisted, too.

Just like these wreaths I was making.

"Oh good, you're almost done," my mother said sitting beside me on the step of the Chanters' porch. "We need so many for a wedding. I don't know why the Earthmovers would plan one when it is almost winter, but we all feel a bit on edge lately and I guess they'd like things settled."

I still wasn't used to her looking ten years older, ten years more broken. The life was coming back to her eyes under her carefully calm exterior, but if I looked at her when she didn't know I was looking, I could see the hot pain roiling under the surface, the long-mulled depression that was hard for her to break.

She'd lost us all for ten years. She'd been widow and the mother of twin disgraces. I didn't know how awful that might be. I tried to imagine it the first night I was back, but just the imagining hurt too much and I shied away from it. It was easier to deal with if I tried to act like nothing had happened in those ten years.

"How's Dad?" I asked.

She cleared her throat. She liked talking about him even though we both knew the truth. She smiled slightly as she spoke.

"He's healthier than he was. Those wounds are closed. Goodie Herben is deft with herbs and the infection won't be back. Maybe soon he'll start remembering things."

I tried not to think too much about that, either. My father remembered my mother. That was a relief. And that first night when he woke from his nightmares and I heard his cry of recognition I'd thought everything was going to be okay.

He remembered Olen's dad and mom. And that was good, too. Because my mother had been living with them these past ten years since we lost our home to the angry villagers and she lost her family to the Fae. They'd even let me stay here since I returned. Or rather, Olen's mother had. His father didn't say much of anything. He just played or sang all the time, one song blending seamlessly into the next and the next. He was playing right now in his rocking chair behind us on the porch as we did our part for the community and wove wreaths for the wedding.

My father didn't remember me or Hulanna. Or anyone born after he married his lovely bride Genda – my mother. He didn't remember raising us or going to the Faewald to go get us. He spent most of his time staring off into space, speaking when he was spoken to, and smiling sweetly at my mother and breaking my heart every time he looked at me with puzzled eyes.

This was not the happy ending I had been looking for.

None of this was supposed to be what I came back to. None of it.

Wreath. Writhe. Wraith. Wrath.

I twisted the last willow branches into an angry wreath.

We'd be at the wedding with the rest of the town – we poor fools who life had passed by. I couldn't help but think of my own wedding, though I'd told no one about it. I'd been tricked into it, after all, so it wasn't like I was going to plan a party for it or have people tie endless wreaths for me.

I should have known that was what the Knave was doing when he tangled that stupid green bandage all around my hands. After all, hadn't I seen green marriage ribbons in our town a thousand times before? Hadn't I seen the village elders tangle them around the hands of the betrothed and tie them together as the two muttered shy "I do's"?

I'd said "I do," and so had Scouvrel. I just hadn't realized what it meant at the time.

I wasn't sure if I was angrier at him for marrying me without my permission or for not telling me about it until it was too late for me to pitch a fit. Coward. I was going to gut him and make a wreath out of his innards.

Except that I wasn't.

Because I was stuck here.

And because it hurt to think about him.

"Can you bring the wreaths to the town square, Allie?" my mother asked with a gentle smile.

I dropped my wreath on the step and leaned in to give her a fierce hug, ignoring the choking sound in her throat.

"Of course," I said, sniffling back tears I refused to shed. She was shaking in my arms and I knew she was thinking all the things she wasn't saying – things about lost years and broken husbands and daughters who were still just seventeen when her friends' children had children now.

But we didn't talk about those things – as if we were both afraid of shattering if we said them out loud, so instead, I just hugged her extra tight before I got up from the steps with feigned enthusiasm, gathered up the twenty wreaths I'd made, tied them quickly with a length of twine and slung them over one shoulder and my backpack over the other.

"See you tonight?" my mother asked, her breath hitching at the end of the sentence and I nodded with more certainty than I felt. She didn't need to know that I would try to go through the circle again before I came home – just like I did every night. After all, I'd probably fail again – just like I did every night.

Chapter Two

My blindfold was secure and with both my hands occupied carrying wreaths and my bag, I couldn't pull it down to check the glowing paths like I usually did, but my feet itched to check them. I knew they all led somewhere, just like the one that had led to the cage I kept tied to my belt at all times and the one that had led to the key I kept in a pouch hanging from a cord around my neck.

I needed to follow the other paths, too. I just hadn't had the chance yet. There were too many eyes on me now. People watched me constantly. I'd heard a whispered "changeling" more than once when I passed a knot of people. I needed to stay unsuspicious so they could trust me again.

I strode down the path from Chanters' house to the wide North Road. There were already eyes on me as I hurried to the village. I waved cheerily to Branchtrimmer who was pulling a cart loaded with cut lengths of wood. He gave me a slow nod, his eyes never leaving my blindfold. He was wary of me. They all were.

I'd been home a solid week and they were still worried about whether I was human or some changeling from a story. I'd cut my hand the first few times to show them I could bleed – I had no idea why they thought that was a good test. The Fae could bleed. I'd seen it. But I didn't want to tell them that and you couldn't cut your hand for every person in the village. I was just getting used to all the suspicious looks. It probably didn't help that I kept my pack with me at all times, like a vagabond. But I'd had too many surprises. I didn't want to be caught without supplies. And I didn't want anyone to find the rat pelt inside – the one as large as a bear hide. People were sure to find that suspicious.

I strode down the path, letting feigned confidence make my steps light and brisk. Nothing to see here. Nothing to see here.

My blindfold slipped down from one eye and I stumbled slightly before I caught myself. I still had trouble looking at the world like that – one eye seeing what seeing people saw and one mostly blind with only spirit residues to guide it.

With my spirit vision, I saw an owl-griffin – tiny and so very Fae – fly by. My head whipped around to watch it go. I looked around, anxious, but no one on the path seemed to notice it or me. Ten years. Ten years for the Fae creatures to become accustomed to these woods. What trouble were they up to out there? My eyes narrowed at the thought. I would need to investigate what damage these Fae creatures were doing to the local animal populations.

And if I could capture one, that might be interesting, too.

At the edge of town, a pair of Olen's guards leaned against posts with a painted pole that they raised and lowered for any carts coming through. They glanced over me and wrote in a book they kept beside the pole.

That was a change.

There were far too many changes.

I couldn't help the tight feeling in my chest at the sight of them. They were strangers to me, and I to them. And that meant that in some strange way, I was a stranger in the only place I'd ever thought of as home. It had grown without me and been claimed by people who weren't me.

I could feel it in the woods, too.

This place that had once been as familiar as my own body felt like a stranger to me now. It made my belly twist and my heart feel hollow.

"Allie!"

The sound of hooves smacking the soft earth still surprised me. That hadn't been a sound you heard very often in the old Skundton, but now I heard horses all the time.

Olen rode up on a snorting horse, its breath hanging in the cool late-autumn air. The horse rolled an eye at me and danced to the side. I shifted my load enough to free a hand and pull my blindfold back up.

"Easy, Blossom, easy," Olen said, patting the mare's side with his hand. I still felt a sharp pain when I saw him, even after a year. He had grown into his gangly frame. He was a full-grown man. And here I was still a girl. I was out of step with the whole world. "I don't know why you make her so nervous."

"Maybe she's heard I'm the village hunter," I said, giving the mare my best side-eye. Our dislike was mutual. Every time I saw her, I thought of the unicorns of the Faewald and their rotting flesh hanging from ethereal skeletons.

Olen laughed awkwardly. "You know the town disposed of that role, Allie. I'm the Knight here, and that's the person who defends the town. We don't need to hunt to eat. We've brought up sheep and chickens, cows and goats. And we don't need a Hunter for defense. Every able-bodied man in Skundton is part of my militia. You really don't need to carry that bow around."

I hitched the wreaths higher on my shoulder and scowled as they rubbed against my quiver and bow. I wasn't giving up my bow and arrows. Not for Olen. Not for anyone.

"You're a young girl, Allie. Let *us* protect you. We all feel bad about what happened to your family."

"Sure," I said, letting my voice drip with sarcasm.

He was talking down to me.

Again.

Just like last night when I'd come into his parents' house to find him in front of the fire stretched out in a chair sipping tea.

"Heldra and I have found a place for you, Allie," he'd said with a smile. "My parents' house is crowded and while I know my mother loves the company, you need to live your life now that you're back."

"I'll start rebuilding our home tomorrow," I'd said awkwardly. I had no idea how to rebuild but I hated living with the Chanters, too. I needed my own space.

Olen shook his head. "We had to take that land to expand the pasture for the Herder's cows. No, Heldra and I were talking about situating you with the Rootdiggers. Aden's wife is pregnant with their seventh child and she could use the help."

"You want *me* to care for children?" I'd asked him, horrified. What parent in their right mind would want a bloodthirsty nightmare like me to care for their little ones? "I'm terrible with children. I make them cry."

"Edrina could use the help. She was your friend. Remember?"

As if I could forget! It might be ten years to them, but it had barely been two seven-days since I'd been young with all of them right here.

"Hulanna's friend," I corrected, because what else was there to say?

"Either way," he'd said, smiling like he was proud of himself. "It will suit everyone perfectly."

Except for me.

I hadn't bothered to say no. I'd just stormed out into the windy night and gone up to the circle, crying and clutching the key as I begged it to open for me.

I'd stayed there all night and when I returned with the light of dawn this morning and my mother had handed me a knife with a hollow smile and told me to make wreaths for the wedding.

Which I had done.

Like a good girl.

What more did they want?

The tiny part of my mind that sounded a lot like Scouvrel these days was laughing because it knew very well what they wanted – they wanted someone other than me. They wanted the girl Hulanna had been before she went into the circle. They wanted a girl like Edrina with her seven children.

They did not want Allie, the difficult one. The one who couldn't stop thinking about a certain Fae and his one single ear.

"Thank you for your concern," I told Olen stiffly. "It must be a fine thing to be a Knight."

His smile was far too bright and his tone too sober. Someone needed to drown *him* in wine. That would take his edge off.

"It's a great honor. One I am determined to live up to."

"You know I'm not moving in with Edrina, right?" I asked, lifting a brow. We were almost to the town square where I could set down these wreaths. And then I was going to follow one of those magic trails and see what I could see.

"You're a part of our town, Allie," Olen said. There was a glimmer of something in his shiny breastplate. It looked – for just a moment – like Scouvrel, his face utterly shocked before his expression turned to delight.

My heart started pounding like I'd seen a buck in the woods. I swallowed and pushed down the excitement. He wasn't here. It was just my imagination.

For a response to Olen, I looked around pointedly at the town that looked nothing like the one I left. At the three bustling inns and the cobbled square. Someone had built a roof over that well in the middle and installed a fancy crank handle to pull up the water more quickly. I didn't recognize even half of the tall homes with thatched roofs – one even had tiles! Or the new smithy, or the sheer size of the butcher's shop. It was like a different town.

I certainly didn't fail to notice the fine house made of stone in the center of town with the little stone walls around the tight yard and Olen's fancy tabards strung along the washline in the back. Beside the house was a long, low stone house that seemed to be both barracks and jail. Someone was doing well with all these changes and that someone was Knight Chanter over here.

"Am I, Olen?" Scouvrel's face really was in his breastplate. His lips formed the words, 'It works.' My own eyes went large as I focused on it through the blindfold.

"I remember Olen," I heard in silken tones just at the edge of my hearing. "He thought he could keep you caged in that little town. What delightful near-sightedness. You should tell him that we are wed. Wouldn't that be fun?"

I was hearing things. This wasn't real. I shook my head to clear it. I *would not* go insane like my father.

Olen frowned. He didn't like me using his name. Probably because I reminded him of where he came from – a tiny nothing town just like me. And where he might have gone – married to me with scowling red-haired children instead of to Heldra with beautiful rosy-cheeked children. All thriving and healthy except for one missing boy.

"Of course you are, Allie, and we remember our own. Heldra thought that perhaps you were insulted by the offer to help Edrina. She said a woman wants her own home."

I grunted noncommittally. I wanted my ten years back, my sister defeated before she could march an army through that magic circle, and the missing children of my home returned. Was that really so much to ask for? I wanted everyone in my family safe and not a danger to this around them. Having a home of my own was pretty low on that list – especially since they were grazing cattle on the land that was *definitely mine.*

Oh, and I wanted to see Scouvrel's face when I turned up and demanded answers about this whole marriage nonsense. I wanted him to explain why he'd thought that was a good idea. That's what I wanted.

"I added that to my letter to Sir Eckelmeyer this morning. I thought that perhaps you might feel awkward marrying one of the village boys your age since they were all little children when you ... ahem ... left us." He looked very grave as he continued, failing to notice how my jaw had dropped. "And of course, it would be very strange for one of us who were once your peers to marry you." I had a sudden memory of walking into his bedroom as he clutched his blankets around his naked body. It was hard not to grin. "Ten years is a very long time and we've all moved on. Even if we weren't all married ourselves. Which is why I proposed he send one of his more promising squires to assist me here and serve as a bridegroom for you."

"You did *what*?" Ugh. I hated how my voice went so high pitched when I was upset. I'd hurt my ears with that shriek.

Olen planted a hand on his hip and looked down at me from the back of Blossom in a way that might have looked imperious if his horse hadn't snorted just then.

"I am making arrangements to procure for you a husband and a home. I'm surprised to find you so ungrateful, Alastra Hunter. This is a great honor for you."

"I'm already married," I said dryly, and I could have sworn I saw Scouvrel snickering in that breastplate.

He wasn't the only one. I couldn't help the tiny wicked grin blossoming on my face as I strode away to deposit my wreaths with the others woven by the Goodies who were decorating the town square. I couldn't help but look once over my shoulder at Olen as he sat frozen on his horse, shock leaving his mouth wide open.

"That's not funny, Allie!" he called after a long moment.

But it actually really was funny.

At least my marriage had been good for *that*.

Chapter Three

Another owl-griffin! These things were everywhere. They must reproduce like rabbits. They'd taken over the niche filled by weasels and martens and the like, killing squirrels and rabbits with reckless abandon.

Someone needed to manage these invaders, or they were going to destroy the weasel and marten populations. But how would they manage a species that they couldn't see? I crouched on the path spreading breadcrumbs in a trail to me, trying to lure them in. So far, no luck. Maybe they were strictly carnivorous.

The desire to be Hunter again left a constant itch on the back of my neck. I could try snaring them.

That's not you anymore, Allie, I had to remind myself. You'd be better off taming one for a pet. At least no one would be furious with you for that. And I might enjoy getting to know a Fae creature – though in its own world it was likely a haunted mess like the unicorn had been.

It was hard to deal with the bitterness that came back every time I was reminded of my lost home and role here. Fuel, Allie. Burn it as fuel, too. This battle isn't over and it's going to need all your concentration. A hunter is, above all things, patient.

I did not feel patient today.

The path I was following had taken me so far to the west that I was well past anywhere I'd ever been before. This far west was all downhill – but not like rolling, lovely hills I'd heard about in the valley kingdoms. This kind of 'downhill' was rocky ravines and paths only a goat – or better yet, an eagle – would ever take.

I was glad for my pack. I'd already made use of the rope and the water skin and I'd resorted to tying the rat hide around me like a cloak. It blocked the wind well and I was not above hiding in a rat hide against the wind.

Another ghoul moaned from the bushes nearby. For Pete's, sake. They couldn't have recruited a Hunter to replace us and keep this ghoul population down? Really?

I felt a twinge of guilt stab through me. There shouldn't have had to be someone to replace us. We should have been here. Knights were all well and good and I could see why the town wanted one to defend against the Fae. Even one like Olen who was a condescending snot these days, but only a Hunter would keep ghouls at bay and the ghoul population had become utterly ridiculous since I left.

"Back, you wraiths!" I yelled, shooting at one that darted toward me for the fourth time in the past hour. They were far too daring – particularly in the light of day. And I was struggling to recover my arrows on a landscape that was more vertical than horizontal.

I pulled my blindfold down again and followed the glowing green path. It edged around a rockslide in a way that made my stomach queasy, but at least it was something to *do*. I was so tired of sitting in that sad house listening to Chanter sing and play day and night, watching my father's haunted eyes, noting the longsuffering patience in the steady work of my mother and Goodie Chanter's hands as they toiled over stove or in garden.

Something moved at the edge of my second sight vision. I turned toward it, but there was nothing there. Hmm. I pulled up my blindfold and shot another arrow at one of the nearby ghouls.

"Fae take you!"

It was the best place to channel my frustration and heartbreak. After all, they didn't belong to this place anymore than I did.

I pulled the blindfold up, recovered the arrow from the fading ghoul and then pulled it down again to find the path. This had better lead somewhere.

Anywhere.

I didn't want to go home empty-handed.

I needed weapons and I needed a plan. A good plan. I'd been dealing with my sister and Scouvrel being a step ahead of me this whole time, but if I could just think like a hunter – if I could imagine where my prey would walk and set snares for them there – then for once I could be ahead instead of behind.

I needed that. I needed it so badly.

I turned the corner around the rock pile and stopped abruptly – a covered wagon lying on its side, long abandoned, the back doors flapping in the howling wind. The glow ended here.

I froze, watching the wagon cautiously. Something might be living in it. A bear or a mountain lion ... or worse. I pulled up my blindfold but there were no tracks in the soft earth around the wagon, no scent of an animal. Carefully, I nocked another arrow and slid through the shadows toward the half-ruined wagon.

It looked like it had tumbled from the paths above, but that had to be a long time ago. Grass and small trees had grown up surrounding it, one of the trees was thick as two of my thumbs but it curved around the wagon as if it had grown like that. It was a long way from any road.

Hmmm.

The cloth covering the wagon had been brightly painted, but it was faded now and ragged, some of the hoops holding it in place bent or shattered.

I waited, easing my blindfold down and then back up again three times and watching carefully every time but there was nothing more to see without getting closer. No trap had sprung. No new creature had emerged.

Something flickered again on the edge of my second sight. I could almost swear it had been something alive. Maybe those owl griffins were playing games with me again.

Swallowing, I crept closer to the wagon, careful to keep tension on my bowstring. If trouble came, I was ready.

A bird squawked, jumping up from the grass beside the wagon and flapping toward me. I bit back a scream and my arrow loosed. The bird was so fast that I had to duck, and even then, I felt its wings brush against my face. My arrow twanged, stuck into the wagon.

You're too jumpy, Allie. I collected my arrow, my cheeks growing hot. It was just a bird, Allie. Just a partridge.

But when I closed my eyes, all I could see was Ghadrot holding my cage and telling me about a Feast of Ravens. They'd be coming soon. Maybe tomorrow. Maybe not for ten years. But they would be coming with an army bent on conquering the Mortal Court – which was my world.

One way or another – whether now or later, they would have to be stopped and a Knight like Olen with a tiny militia of townsfolk wouldn't be enough to stop them. And neither would this Sir Eckelmeyer or any squire he might send to wed me. Even if I weren't already married, I didn't dare start a family. Not when they were liable to be slaughtered before my eyes.

I gritted my teeth in anger, crossed the rest of the way to the wagon and snatched the cloth aside. The mouth of the wagon bed was dark. I ducked and stepped inside as the door swung in the wind and hit me on the backside.

I stumbled forward, thinking I would hit the back of the tangled mess of a wagon. Instead, I stumbled through bright light and into a ring of surprised people.

What in all the ...?

I looked behind me at a solid oak tree as fat as three of me were wide.

I blinked.

"You found the door, deary. And with a blindfold on and all. Of course, it's the cloth of sight, so you'd be seeing just fine with it."

I spun to see the woman addressing me. She smirked at my surprise. She was my mother's age with wings of white hair over her ears, the rest of it blacker than a raven wing. And though her eyes were hard and glittering, her smile was warm, and her clothing was a strange assortment of every kind and color.

I clenched my jaw to keep myself from saying something stupid. Instead, I let my eyes wander around the circle at the others with her – men and women and children, babies so young they were slung in bright cloth over their mothers' breasts, and every other age. The colors they wore hurt my eyes

– blues so bright they dulled the sky were set beside oranges so rich that they made wildflowers look shy. Reds and yellows that rivaled the brightest birds I'd ever seen and blacks darker and richer than the shadows of the Faewald.

They were Travelers, as my mother's mother had been. And their covered wagons sat in a ring around the tree I'd stepped out of. A big ring. I could count thirty from where I stood and between them, there were more. Many more.

"And what do you call yourself, girl?" the one who had spoken before spoke again.

"Allie Hunter," I said clearly. Best to be respectful.

"And you keep to the old ways? Follow the paths?"

"What paths?"

Her eyebrows rose. "Well, you came through the door, so I just thought ..." She let the thought hang in the air. It seemed to be waiting for me to say more.

"I followed an orange glowing trail and it led me to a fallen wagon and when I entered it, I found myself here."

She nodded gravely. "Then know, Archer, that we are a permanent encampment set up here to trade with others like us as they pass through this place. We lend aid to those in need and shelter the helpless. In all our travel, this is the one place we've found safety for our people and our old ways. The door you entered will let no evil pass."

"That's nice," I said and her mouth tightened with disapproval. What did she want from me?

"Secrecy is essential for our safety."

I nodded.

"Which means we can't let you leave unless you swear se-crecy and that you will only ever return if you are bringing the helpless to us to be kept safe."

"What if I'm helpless and I need you?" I asked.

Her laugh was harsh. "You could be naked in a snowstorm surrounded by ghouls, girl, and you would still not be helpless."

Well, it was nice to be appreciated.

"In that case," I said, "I so swear. And I suppose I'll be leaving?"

They all nodded as if they had expected that. Well. What a waste of time. I should have stayed home and tied more wreaths.

I turned and walked toward the oak tree. Here's hoping it would at least take me home.

"Wait a moment," the woman with the white wings in her hair said. "My name is Denera and I am the Loremistress of our camp."

I nodded, not sure what else to do other than to put my bow and arrow away. I did so a little sheepishly.

"Good to meet you," I said, looking around awkwardly before shrugging, striding to the oak tree, and gently leaning into it

I stumbled through to the other side and stood in the dark covered wagon, panting as I caught my breath.

I'd hoped for a weapon or some way to get into the Fae-wald. Instead, I'd found a useless path to the Travelers. What could they do about the Fae? My ancestors had let me down.

I paused for a moment. Maybe they could take my parents and keep them safe there. Although they weren't in danger yet. Not until our town was invaded again. But we'd have no warning. We'd have no way to get out before they arrived. I needed to start working on getting my parents out of town – on getting everyone out of town.

And I needed weapons. I needed another key. Or another book. Or a big sword for hacking the Court of Twilight into pieces. Or something. Anything but secret broken wagons and howling ghouls.

I paused, realizing that I'd met those people while wrapped in a rat skin. Maybe I should just be glad that they hadn't attacked me. I probably looked terrifying.

I shook my head and began the slow work of following the trail home. I'd try another trail tomorrow and I'd figure out a plan.

If Scouvrel was here, he'd already be making a game out of this. 'Truth or Lie,' he'd say. 'You're terrible at getting what you need.' And then I'd have to tease him about how I'd sold him for what I needed.

But that didn't feel very funny. Neither was the idea of me marrying a squire.

If he had been here, he would have bargained with me to reopen that circle. He would have helped me with a plan to snare the coming Fae army.

But he wasn't here. And the stone circle remained closed. And until it opened again, I was nothing more than a simple village girl with tattoos she had to keep hidden from sight and crazy ideas about a coming war.

I needed to think. There had to be a way to snare them. And I had to find it on my own.

Chapter Four

What I needed, I decided, was to think things through. It was easier to think out here with my blindfold off, following the orange trail of the spirit path back to my home. I had to stop often to pull the blindfold back up again, but at least that was my only distraction – that and the iron cage that I kept tied to my belt. It knocked against my leg as I walked, but I was beginning to feel the rhythm of it and that helped it stay in the background.

If I was my sister, what would I do?

She sent scouts first last time. It stood to reason that she might send some again.

Which meant I needed to watch for those.

Something flickered on the edge of my vision again and I whipped my head around, but all I saw was the glowing trail and the swooping owl griffins set against a dark, nebulous background of the forest in my spirit vision.

Was it just owl griffins, or was there something more out there? A phoenix perhaps, or a unicorn? Whatever it was, I should catch it by surprise. All I needed was one more glimpse of that flicker and I could put it in my cage if it was a Fae creature. Which is probably what I should have done with the owl griffins, now that I thought about it. I could have a whole cage of those things buzzing around by now.

Don't get distracted, Allie. Focus.

Okay. I stood still, pulled my blindfold up, blinked at the real world, and then whipped it down again and spun. The spirit world rushed by in all it's flickering, wavering glory. I saw the flicker and I immediately focused.

You are small. You are nothing. You can fit in my cage with ease.

I heard a curse from the cage and with my heart in my throat, I held it up.

Disappointment filled me.

Had I been hoping that Scouvrel would be sent out as a scout again? I must have been, or else I would have been thrilled, because standing in my cage, hissing angrily, was the beautiful orc Lieutenant who had told me all about tricks of marriage.

"Lieutenant," I said with a smile. "It's good to see you again."

"I hate your dull world with its bland colors and ugly people," she spat.

"Well, at least you aren't prone to flattery," I replied, my eyebrow lifting. I had to be sly and cool. I didn't dare let her know how much my heart was racing. "How many of you are there out in my woods?"

"Just me," she said with a sneer. "An insulting job, but your Lord Cavariel is not a male known for his value of females."

"Man," I corrected.

"Does the word 'male' bother you?" she asked, looking interested.

"The suggestion that people are nothing more than their sex does."

She laughed. "And what are you going to do with me now that I'm in your cage, Rat Killer?"

I swallowed. I hadn't thought that far.

"I'm going to send you back to the Faewald," I said.

"Great. I'm sick of scouting this place and I've seen all I need to see."

Oh great, Allie. You've backed yourself into a corner now!

"Like what?" I countered and she laughed. Despite the cold, she wore only a black leather corset, fish-skin breeches, and a fish-skin jacket so short it covered only her shoulders and chest. She stood easily in the center of the cage, a bronze throwing axe in each hand. Uh oh. I hoped she didn't' try to attack with those. Even in miniature, they would hurt.

"Like how pathetic your knight and his so-called militia are," she said with a laugh.

I did not dare let her go back.

"You're staying with me," I said grimly.

"To what end?"

"You're going to help me set a trap for your armies."

"Unlikely." Her tone was disinterested.

But I would find a way. And I would trap them all.

Chapter Five

By the time I wandered into the Chanters' kitchen – cluttered and filled with odds and ends just like their house had always been – it was past dawn. I brought eggs in from the hens and a bucket of water – the least I could do.

I had the Lieutenant in the cage at my belt, grateful that no one could see her without my spirit vision. I'd given her my handkerchief to sit on so that the iron didn't burn her, but she'd taken it in slit-eyed, stony silence.

My mother took the eggs silently, her eyes wary as she poured the water into the kettle and laid the eggs into a basket. Beside the fire, my father sat wrapped in blankets and muttering to himself.

"One in two, and two to be one. Rip and mend. Tear and treat. Open and close. Sow and reap."

You could go crazy listening to him. Maybe my mother *was* going crazy listening.

"Come now, Chanter, let's clean you up for the wedding," I heard Goodie Chanter saying on the porch.

My mother shot a furtive look in her direction before leaning close to me. "You can't spend every night up there, Allie. People are going to notice. I can only cover for you so often."

I didn't bother denying it. I had slept in my tent at the circle when I came back from my strange adventure walking through wagons and oak trees. It had seemed like the best place for me. I was neither of one world nor the other, after all. And it gave me a chance to interrogate my prisoner, which hadn't worked at all. She hadn't even been willing to part with her name.

"They're coming, Mother," I whispered. They wouldn't send a scout if they weren't. "And there is no Chanter or Hunter now."

"There are Knights, Allie," my mother said gently. "The world changes and we change with it."

"And what if I don't want to change?"

My mother seemed to sag. "Ah, daughter. I don't want you to change, either." She sighed. "But all of this changed without you. The town changed. The people changed. I changed. I didn't mean to, Allie, but loneliness and grief hollow a person and I'm hollow, Allie. I'm nothing but a shell." She was crying now. Gently. Tears leaking down her face. I gathered her into my arms and she leaned her forehead on my shoulder, whispering as she cried. "I'm as bad as your father. Worse, because his mind is drifting away but mine is still here and it's only my hope that is gone."

"What would get it back for you, Mom?" I whispered. "I'll do whatever I need to do."

"I'm worried about your sister. You haven't spoken of her which must mean ... did she die, Allie? Is she gone?"

From the cage, the Lieutenant snorted.

"No. She's the one leading the army planning to invade our land."

My mother hissed, pulling back from the hug and looking frantically around the room before leaning close to me. "Don't let anyone hear you say that."

I nodded, widening my eyes as if to say, 'obviously.'

"Allie," she said, her eyes wild now. "I have to stop her. She's my daughter, my responsibility!"

"No!" The word ripped out of me before I could stop it. The thought of my mother being snatched by my sister – of her being tortured and hurt – it made something in my heart burn.

She slammed a finger against her lips, looking frantically toward the porch where Goodie Chanter was still cooing to her mad husband.

I brought my voice back down to a whisper. "Someone has to tend Father. He might still get his mind back. He might just need a little time."

I was pleading, I knew that, and I could see her agreement in the way her lower lip trembled, and she glanced back at my father by the fire.

"You know I'm not fit to nurture anything," I whispered with a teasing tone. "Hulanna always took care of the baby goats. I was out trapping marten and fox."

My mother nodded, her eyes glassy with tears and the tip of her nose reddening over her wry smile. I let my expression sharpen with determination.

"So, let me do what I do best. Let me hunt my sister. Let me bring her down. You said she was our responsibility. Well, I'll take that responsibility, and you take this one." I nodded to my father.

Her pause was long and heavy but after a moment she nodded. "You are better at hunting."

"I am."

"How will you do it?" she asked.

"I don't know yet. But I'll find a way."

The door opened with a bang as the wind shook it and Goodie Chanter bustled into the room with her husband whistling behind her.

"Oh, Allie, you're a wreck! Twigs in your hair and clothes rumpled! There's to be a wedding today! Go fix yourself, girl."

"Thanks, Goodie Chanter," I said with a false smile.

Best to try to be grateful. After all, she'd taken my mother in when the town was against us. And now she'd taken my father in, too. That had to be hard on her – two women who were basically widows tending madmen while trying to manage their cottage and livestock together. I should feel guilty that I wasn't planning to stay and help. I rubbed my arm with my hand, feeling the claws of guilt sneak up and pierce me – but not enough to change my course.

"Your mother found a dress for you. You should put it on quickly. We've only an hour before the wedding. Look at yourself!"

She shoved a small mirror – carefully polished silver and the size of my palm – into my hand. I glanced down and nearly dropped it. In the mirror, I saw Scouvrel's face staring back.

He gasped.

"Haunt me, Nightmare," he pled. "Haunt me until I beg you to stop."

There was snickering from the cage.

I looked around, terrified that my mother and Goodie Chanter had heard, but all Goodie Chanter did was take the mirror from my hand gently.

"See? Even you are surprised at your own reflection!"

I was going as insane as my father. I was seeing Scouvrel everywhere. I shook my head.

Get a hold of yourself, Allie! Do normal things.

Which was how I found myself an hour later with my wild red hair tamed back into a long braid and my bow and quiver slung over a simple homespun dress with a carefully stitched corset and fur-lined cloak.

Where my mother had found them was beyond me but she'd outdone herself with adapting them to fit me – though she'd leaned in when she gave them to me whispering that I should be careful to hide those "Fae marks" on my body or people would grow anxious. Kind as that was, I couldn't help the ache that formed in my chest as I slipped the clothing on.

I missed Scouvrel's elaborate clothing made of feathers and arrogance. Everything in the mortal world felt dull in comparison. Clean. Pure. But dull. Perhaps even a few days in the Faewald had been enough to taint me forever.

"You're not taking that cage with you, Allie?" Goodie Chanter had asked me, shocked to see it hanging from my belt again. "What on earth would you need that for?"

"Maybe I'll catch butterflies," I suggested. "I can't do that without it."

"You'll certainly never catch a man *with* it," she'd replied.

As if I wanted to *catch* a man. Even if I wasn't accidentally married, I was pretty sure I had more interesting things to catch. Like the laughing Lieutenant in the cage. Now, if I could only make her talk ...

The bride and groom – Aiden and Jenne – stood at the front of the assembly as the town elders wrapped a green ribbon around their hands and led them through their vows, but my mind was not on their sweet exchange. My eyes were roving over the people assembled here. Even with all the new additions to the town, there were barely more than five hundred people in Skundton and at least half of those were children. I swallowed to clear my dry throat as I watched children and more children huddling against the skirts of mothers or leaning out of the high windows of the new houses lining the town square. If violence came here it would be that laughing little boy in the window who was hurt – or those two sisters holding hands and swaying back and forth with flowers in their hair.

Something had to be done about this. I couldn't let these innocent people suffer because of my family's mistakes.

But the last time I'd tangled with my sister she had guessed my every move before I'd made it. She'd bested me every single time. I couldn't let that happen this time. This time, I had to lure her out of the place where she was powerful and trap *her* instead of the other way around.

The first thing was to determine what she wanted.

The second was to gather weapons to fight.

The third was to make her nervous.

The fourth was to set an irresistible trap.

The fifth was to spring it and catch her.

If Scouvrel was here, he would know how to do that. He'd know what she wanted. I felt an itch between my shoulder blades at the thought of him. If I hadn't accidentally bargained him away, he would be here now with all that knowledge of his. And what would he say?

He'd say she wanted the mortal world for herself, so setting a trap meant setting it here. I'd need to find the right place here to lure her to and I needed a trap ready for when she got here.

He'd say that I needed to follow the other trails to see if there were any other weapons I could use against her. And that made sense. Maybe I'd get lucky and one of them would have a pipe for calling in errant sisters. I already had the trap. If this cage could hold Scouvrel, a unicorn, and the Lieutenant, it could hold Hulanna.

Around me, the town broke out in a whoop of celebration, throwing the last goldenrod of autumn up into the air and letting the icy winds blast it in swirls of golden flowers around us. The wedding was over. The feast was beginning.

Roast goose and apples were brought out, their fragrant scents making my mouth water as the pastries and mead followed.

I snatched two pastries from a waiting tray, shoving one between the cage bars – I wasn't heartless.

But as I looked around at the people I'd known all my life, they seemed like strangers to me. Who was that flushed teenage girl laughing over mulled wine with the boy a head taller than her stammering an apology? Who was that old woman cheering the bride and groom or the man beside her juggling a toddler on his knee and a huge tankard in his other hand? These people were just regular people and they lived right beside a magical circle that was going to open soon and swallow them whole.

I shivered.

Unease swirled in my belly and, frustrated, I stormed out of the town and into the forest beyond, gratified when a partridge flew up at the sound of my boots on the ground. At least in the forest, everything understood what was real – that we were all predators or prey, or both. That eating in peace and marrying in a shower of flowers was horrifically foolish. All of this could be snatched in a moment – would be snatched if someone didn't do something about it.

I ripped off my blindfold.

"Tell me what my sister is going to do, Lieutenant. Make a bargain with me for your freedom."

She smirked at me but chose to stay silent.

I growled between my teeth and chased down the first glowing path that I saw. There had to be an advantage out here somewhere, and I was going to find it, with or without the Lieutenant's help.

Chapter Six

It was well past dark by the time I found the end of the path. My dress was ripped and dirty and I was freezing cold. I should have stopped to change and grab my things before I went charging out in the night. I should have stopped to think, but oh no, of course I just went haring off into the woods like the blind fool I was.

Strange sounds filled the nights – not just the howl of ghouls but the hoots of the owl-griffins and the chatter of some other Faerie creature that glowed a slight magenta and flitted from tree to tree in little swarms that liked to follow me through the woods. I didn't like this haunted wood. It was not my home.

And I was blind out here. In order to follow the path, I'd had to keep the blindfold off. And that meant a lot of stumbles, a lot of scraped knees and cut hands. I'd moved from frustration to anger to despair. And here I was at the end of the glowing red path that led to a hollow tree.

"You've spent a lot of time falling today, Mortal," the Fae in the cage said, finally breaking her silence.

I held it up so I could look at her. "I think we should strike a bargain, Lieutenant."

"You have nothing that I want."

"Not even your freedom?"

"You won't free me here."

"And what if I free you in the Faewald? What then? Would you bargain with me? Would you tell me something of my sister's plans to invade this world?"

"I can tell you that you're a fool," she said, baring her teeth at me in a snarl. "That's free. You don't even need to bargain for it."

"I'm unaccustomed to Fae who won't bargain," I said, frustrated.

"That's because you've been dealing with the Knave and with the Court of Cups. In the Court of Twilight, we bargain more rarely. We have no need of others or anything they might offer us."

"Keep telling yourself that," I muttered. Eventually, she would wear down in that cage and then she would bargain. I had.

I dropped the cage and shoved my head in the tree and looked around with my spirit eyes. Cobwebs brushed my face and I shuddered. That had better not be little legs I felt running down my neck. Oh, sweet stars, it was! Yeck!

I shook like a dog and forced my eyes to stay open. Okay. Forget the spiders. Erg. Try to focus. Was anything glowing? There was something long like an axe handle above me. It glowed a faint red. I grabbed the bottom of it, but it didn't want to budge.

Gritting my teeth, I yanked it back and forth, trying to loosen it from the crumbling worm-eaten wood of the hollow tree. I blinked and cursed as rotten wood fell into my open eyes. Great.

I gave the handle one final tug and with a loud creak, the handle pulled from the tree. Hastily, I scrambled out from the hollow, but something smacked me in the jaw sending me flying backward, hitting a rough stump on my way down and sprawling in the frosty grass. The sounds of three distinct thumps masked anything else.

I yanked my blindfold up, trying to see what happened in the moonlight.

The tree had fallen in three crumbling pieces. One of them must have knocked me back. I should just be glad I wasn't crushed.

"Incompetence," the Lieutenant hissed.

"You can just be quiet if you have nothing productive to contribute," I said, but I was rattled.

Trembling, I lifted the piece of wood. It was the length of my arm and though it was carved to easily fit a hand and smoothed by wear, it didn't seem to have anything special about it. Maybe in better light, I'd see something.

Frustrated, I jammed it in my belt and made the long, cold trek home. I was too discouraged to be excited by the hoots of local owls. Too miserable to enjoy the crisp scent of a world that would soon be decked in snow or to enjoy the pleasant way the tree branches danced like the skirts of a swaying singer.

If this was the best I had, then I was in trouble. One trapped Fae and a length of wood. Amazing work, Allie. You'll be ahead of your sister in no time.

After an hour a pair of ghouls started following me. I let them. I could always scare them off later and they suited my foul mood. It was too dark to see well with the blindfold on and there was no more path with it off. It had disappeared the moment I took the axe handle from the tree. My trek back to the Chanters' house was taking twice the time it should and with nothing to show for it but a long smooth handle.

Honestly, if my ancestors couldn't be bothered to write down what they'd hidden all over the countryside and note what it did then why should I bother going hunting for it all? But I knew the answer. I did it because I didn't have any other clues. This was my only chance to find some way to return to the Faewald for the children there.

With a sigh, I kept going, the ghouls getting closer and closer. I pulled my blindfold down to get a good look at them – at least I could see their spirit forms with the blindfold – and spun, coming face to face with one of the horrific death-heads. It opened its mouth as if it really thought I would get close enough to let it kiss me and take my soul.

I wrenched the axe handle from my belt and swung it at the ghoul and almost dropped it in surprise when the end of the handle flared to life with a crimson burst of flame.

The ghoul shrieked, dashing away and knocking over the other ghoul in its haste. It leapt to its feet joining the first ghoul. Their screeches faded into the night as I lifted the torch, surprised by how bright it was. The flames that danced on the end of the shaft looked very real, and they lit my path like a real torch would, and yet they didn't consume the wood or burn any kind of fuel.

Curious, I pulled my blindfold up with one hand. I was plunged back into darkness.

A spirit torch.

I liked it. At least it could get me home with my spirit vision. It revealed more than my simple blindfold did, lighting the spirit world like the Faewald had been to my second sight.

"I don't know what trick you have played, Mortal, but hiding from me does you no good," the Lieutenant said sharply. Was she nervous?

I looked down at her but her eyes were unfocused, seeming to almost look through me.

"Get some sleep," I told her.

Was it possible that she couldn't see me? That would be an interesting gift to have in a world of Fae.

I could use this torch to light the way home and tomorrow, after I explained away my ripped dress and my absence from the house, I could go chase down another path and another and another until I found all my ancestors' little stashes of odd items. Maybe, eventually, there would be a way to make the key work again and open the Faewald.

The memory of a voice rang in my mind with every step.

"Haunt me, Little Nightmare. Haunt me until I beg you to stop."

I was feeling incomplete without someone to haunt.

Chapter Seven

I woke the next morning with a gasp, scrambling to the kitchen and grabbing a huge frying pan before reaching into the cage carefully and plucking a hair from the sleeping Fae's head.

She screamed, leaping to her feet and throwing her axes through the bars. I'd been ready for that. I threw my hand up, letting them clatter off the back of the cast iron pan.

"What have you done to me?" she shrieked.

It hadn't taken long to collect her axes and replace the pan. It had taken a bit longer to run up to the stone circle in the pre-dawn light.

I stood there, gasping for breath and tingling all over. The first thing I was going to do was find Scouvrel and tell him that now that we were friends forever, he had to help me trap Hulanna.

I took the chunk of hair I'd torn from her head and wound it around the golden key, gathered my pack and all my things, drew in a huge breath and stepped into the circle.

Nothing happened.

I cursed quietly.

"Now do you want to explain why you assaulted a Lieutenant of the Court of Twilight in her sleep, Rat Killer?" she breathed. "I will roast you slowly over a bed of coals. I will season you with ginger and onions. I will watch my court strip your bones."

"Not today you won't," I said, despair heavy on my heart. There will be a way, Allie. Don't give up.

Chapter Eight

Chasing down spirit trails without people thinking you were crazy or getting angry that you were walking through their sheep pen or cattle grazing fields was harder than I'd anticipated. I'd had more clods of earth thrown at me and curses shouted than I cared to count.

I'd also witnessed a cluster of those magenta glowing things with wings pick up a chicken out of its yard and go flying off with it, the owner none the wiser. Two sheep had also been snatched by packs of owl-griffins while I watched from the woods, calm and patient as any hunter would be. I'd considered putting them all in the cage with the Lieutenant, but it had never been my way to torture anything – the Fae woman or the creatures.

The people of Skundton thought they didn't need a Hunter here, did they? And yet, with every passing day I saw how much that wasn't true.

Two weeks of treasure hunting was enough to make me more than a few enemies in the town and produce a grand total of one moldy bow that seemed to have no spirit abilities at all, and a rusty sword likewise bereft of value.

I kept them both in the branches of the eagle nest tree outside the Chanters' house, carefully oiling and re-stringing the bow with a waxed string just in case I could use it someday to the Lieutenant's amusement.

"With such glorious weapons, your victory must seem very near to you," she'd laughed. But that was the most I could get out of her. Mockery. Needling. She would not offer anything else up and she could not be convinced or bargained with. Like me, she was relying on patience to win the day.

Who knew if maybe I'd find out something that made the weapons valuable, despite her mockery? If anyone had learned that magic wasn't always easy to see, it was me.

What I feared most was that they would send more scouts. Or worse, that the army would plunge through the circle before I was ready. I knew what Hullana wanted. I had the trap. But what would I use for bait? And where would I set it?

I kept the axe handle in my belt at all times on a loop I'd sewn for it, alongside the hanging cage. I was becoming a walking magic-tool chest. The light of day hadn't revealed anything new about it – no magical writing or buttons or secret compartments. Nothing that made it look like anything other than a handle with no blade. But all I had to do was lift it with my blindfold off, and it illuminated the spirit world in a way so intense that my heart almost skipped a beat. Better yet, the Lieutenant seemed to lose sight of me when I was using it. Invisibility was a strong skill to have. What would it be like to take it into the Faewald? What would it reveal that even my second sight hadn't seen on its own? I was dying to try it out.

At the end of the two weeks, my mother and Goodie Chanter were both frustrated with me for the mud and rips in my clothing and the late hours I kept.

"At least she isn't taking up space like you feared, Goodie Chanter," I'd overheard my mother saying as she poured tea for the both of them.

"I'd forgotten that raising children who were almost grown was so much work, Genda. You don't think ... you don't think she's carrying on with one of the village boys, do you?"

"Nonsense. They were all children when she left here," my mother said, and I felt a sense of satisfaction at her words. At least someone had confidence in me still.

"Well, then, one of the village *men*? She's filthy and rumpled when she comes home. Could she be stealing kisses behind the barns and in the lofts?" Goodie Chanter had asked. "My Olen, for instance ..."

"No, Danna," my mother said repressively. "Allie is a good girl. She wouldn't bother your boy."

"His marriage to Heldra is happy," Goodie Chanter said, but it sounded more like a warning than a statement.

"Of course, it is, Danna," my mother said, and I shivered.

There was a time when I would have been jealous of Heldra. A time when I would have wanted her life. Now, the thought of stolen kisses reminded me only of Scouvrel and the way his kisses had seared onto my lips leaving them ruined for anyone else.

Fae ruined everything. Those few kisses had left me immune to human men. None of them caught my eye or made my heart beat any faster.

I'd taken my mother and Goodie Chanter's words as license to try just one more time. It couldn't hurt to try just one more time, could it?

Wrong. It could hurt. But I was willing to hurt if that was the only way.

I hiked through the woods and up to the mountain plain, arriving as night descended over the lonely stone circle. No one played music here anymore. There was no hunter set to shoot at strange creatures. There was no defense set at all.

Calmly, I stripped down to my underthings and danced across the frosty ground around the circle.

"Next time you decide to disrobe, be sure and warn me," the Fae in my cage said. "You're even uglier than usual with less to cover you."

I ignored her and danced.

Faster, faster, faster.

The sparkling silver grass crunching under my feet as the moon swelled full and bright and I thought of what I loved about the Faewald – of the huge statue with its eye full of books, of the greenish orc skin of Ghadrot and his toothy grin, of the nest of feathers beside the river and the scent of cedars wafting through the Court of Cups, and of smoke waterfalls and flying through the mountains and of the bright hope in Scouvrel's haunted eyes and the way his lips felt when they brushed mine.

My toe hit a rock and with an angry curse, I tumbled to the ground, skinning both knees. I'd cracked the toenail on the biggest toe of my left foot, and it *hurt*. Making a tiny mewing sound, I wrapped it back up and reluctantly put my clothing back on as the first snowflakes of winter began to drift down into the magic circle. The dead, useless, lifeless magic circle.

Take me, circle. Take me back to the Faewald!

But just like every time before, nothing happened.

Chapter Nine

There was something different about the feel of the town when I trudged through the melting snow bringing our goat cheese to town to trade for flour with strict instructions from Goodie Chanter that I was only to trade with the Baker family and not those new Spencers who had come up to Skundton from the valleys.

"They are not our people," she warned me strictly.

Which seemed silly, because they were mortal which made them more 'our people' than the ones waiting for us beyond the circle I couldn't open.

They were certainly more 'our people' than the person sitting in my cage right now. I'd tried to bargain with her again last night. I'd pled with her. I'd threatened her. I'd tried to tease out some interest from her. She was completely immune to me.

"I can wait, Mortal. My Court will soon rush across your land like termites. Then, they will free me from this cage and present your innards as a prize to me."

I'd given up after that. Which was why I agreed to go to town for Goodie Chanter this morning. I needed the right place to trap Hulanna when she arrived and to pick it, I wanted to spy out the town.

Where would she go first when she arrived? Our old cottage? It was gone now, but that didn't make it a poor choice for setting my trap.

But Hulanna liked an audience. I had a feeling she'd want to come right into the town square.

I huffed my way toward the Bakery, lost in thoughts of how to set a trap for an enemy who might come at any time, who far out-numbered me and had all the advantages. It wasn't until I was almost there that I noticed how quiet the town was.

I froze.

No guards had stopped me at the gates.

There were no children underfoot.

Someone was building a platform in the center of town beside the well. The kind of platform you might stand on to give a speech. They'd left a saw halfway through a length of timber as if they had been interrupted in cutting it.

A chill came over me and I set the wrapped cheese down on the steps of the bakery and ran through the town to the faint sounds in the distance. Something was happening south of Skundton.

I felt for my bow, pulling it free from the quiver and pausing only long enough to string it. My heart was in my throat, my hands shaking already.

They couldn't have come through the circle, could they?

Not with me watching every day and night.

But I was only one person. And I'd been out last night looking for the end of a green trail that looped and spiraled around and around until I lost all hope and stumbled home. I hadn't been to the circle in a full day.

Maybe I'd missed the invasion.

Maybe I'd missed my chance to set my trap.

There were shouts up ahead – not happy squeals of children but angry-sounding shouts. I quickened my pace, trotting down the street past empty houses and shops. A few heads peered curiously from windows and doors, but everyone was still, watching silently as if trying to hear the distant noise.

If this was war, we were woefully unprepared.

I let my fingers run over my arrows as I ran. Twelve. I should have brought more. I should have known better.

The Lieutenant was silent in her cage, not deigning to talk even now. I didn't have time to pull down my blindfold and look at her. If she was using this moment to escape, there was nothing I could do about that now.

The sounds of jeering and shouting were growing louder. I heard something clang and something else like metal hitting wood. I forced my legs to run faster.

There were people up ahead, jammed into a pack. No sight of guards or soldiers. No sign of Olen on his horse. Fat lot of good knights did.

But no, this wasn't an attack. Someone from the back of the crowd threw a cabbage forward. Hardly a winning move in a pitched battle.

And I was beginning to hear words.

"We don't want your kind here! Boo!"

"Go back where you came from!"

"Get out of here!"

Someone spun in the crowd, looking toward me. The wild eyes and anger in his expression gripped my heart. The last time I'd seen a look like that had been on Cavariel's face. It was a look of pure malevolence. A twisted look.

"Let me through!" I demanded, pushing past the angry man and grunting when he elbowed me in the ribs. That had been no accident.

And neither was this mob – because that was what it was. Angry faces, twisted in ways that made them look less than human, pressed in on every side. Men, women, boys, girls, every age and type but all joined in one animal-like emotion.

I clenched my jaw and pushed through them, fearing the worst. Maybe Scouvrel had made it through the stone circle. Maybe he had come looking for me. Something inside ached at the thought. Not my heart, obviously, just my injured toe. Obviously.

And yet my breath was coming too quickly when I finally burst through the crowd to the middle of all the chaos.

Well, here's where the horse was.

Olen sat his brown mare, shouting down at the people while he held the reins of a pair of draft horses. Steam rose from the draft horses as they snorted, their bodies quivering with pent up tension and their eyes rolling so far back that all I could see were the whites. They'd stampede at any minute if someone didn't calm them. Their stomping hooves already cut divots out of the packed earth of the road.

Behind them, a colorful covered wagon draped and wrapped in lilac purple and canary yellow silk cloth, shook with every stomp and tug and a pair of brown eyes – wide with terror – peered at me from a gap between the cloth and the wagon. Someone had painted bright shining suns on the side of the wagon with the abandon of children.

Beside me, someone shook a fist. When I looked back, the eyes darted out of sight. There was a child in there and the crowd was screaming for her blood.

Furious, I pushed through the last of the people, using my own elbows this time.

"Calm down!" Olen roared from the back of the horse.

I ignored him. He was doing this wrong. I strode up to the nose of the first horse, put my hand up to his muzzle and let him sniff it while I whipped off my big cloak and threw it over his head. He needed quiet and to ignore the raging crowd.

The other animal tried to break forward, but I leapt into his path before he could tug the blinded one more than a pace. He towered over me, his massive snout so big that my hand looked like a drifting leaf beside it, but I stretched the cloak to cover his eyes, too, and then leapt up onto his back.

In the driver's seat, a harrowed looking woman clutched the reins, her face lined with worry and beside her, a musta-chioed man held a prod as if he could keep the raging crowd away. Their garish dress told me they were Travelers.

Just like the peaceful Loremistress. Just like my grandmoth-er.

I swallowed. If Skundton had turned on the Travelers, then it was in worse shape than I thought.

"What's the meaning of this?" I bellowed from the horse's back.

Olen's expression was stunned. Hadn't he seen me get up here? But he'd never been the most observant person.

"Get down, Allie Hunter!" someone called from the crowd. "This is no concern of a Fae-lover like you!"

"Fae lover?" I asked, leaning forward with a snarl. "That's what you call me? I, who kept the Fae from destroying this town by sending them back into the circle and closing it behind me? I, who lost my sight to keep you safe?"

Couldn't they see the blindfold covering my eyes? The Travelers could. They were eyeing me with knowing looks. And then their eyes traveled to the cage I always kept tied to my belt, and those eyes widened.

I hoped they couldn't see who was in it.

"I don't believe you *are* blind!" Goodie Rootdigger called, spitting to emphasize her words. "You saw well enough to jump onto those horses!"

"And did you see well enough to see these are Travelers?" I demanded. "Did you fail to see the colorful wagon or the bright silk scarves? We've never threatened Travelers in Skundton! We've always welcomed their stories by our fires and the marvelous things they bring to trade!"

"Times have changed," Olen said quietly and around him the crowd murmured agreement. "Sir Eckelmeyer has decreed all Travelers are to be stopped and detained."

My mouth fell open. "You're arresting these people?"

He looked away, his face flooding an ugly red. He was wearing his shining breastplate like he was a shining knight from a tale come to save us all and not a terrible disappointment.

"Why?" I felt like the breath had been knocked out of me, like I was plummeting down a hole.

"They spread magic!" Goodie Rootdigger called and beside her Goodie Baker muttered agreement.

"There are children in that wagon," I said appalled, planting my free hand on my hip. "Are you going to arrest children, Olen Chanter?"

I turned to fix him with my gaze and he still wouldn't meet my eyes. There were eyes in his breastplate, though. And they met mine just fine.

"Tangled is as tangled does, Little Hunter," Scouvrel said from the reflection on the breastplate. I swallowed and tried not to look. I really was going insane! I was seeing him everywhere.

"You're a child yourself, Allie," Olen said. "What do you know of laws and duties?"

I felt my own cheeks growing hot – but not with shame, like his. I was all fury.

"More than you, it would seem, *Sir* Chanter. I know not to persecute the innocent or harass peaceful people in wagons painted with *sunshines and rainbows*!"

"They're to be detained and their goods and possessions seized," Olen said quietly. The crowd had grown quiet, too. I heard someone drop a coin and heard it roll down the street until it hit a stone wall. It was shockingly clear in the silence around us.

"And then what?" I could hardly see I was shaking so hard. I wanted to hit someone. Preferably, Olen.

"And then he'll feel your wrath," Scouvrel's image said from Olen's breastplate, eyes bright.

Please don't go crazy now, Allie. Get a hold of yourself.

"And then Sir Eckelmeyer will pronounce judgment when he arrives," Olen said stiffly.

"Which will be?" I looked at the Travelers in the cart, looked at the hopeless gazes as if they couldn't even summon the enemy to fight back.

"They love the Fae, Allie," Olen said as if *he* was the one being reasonable. "They trade in magic or with those who do. They don't belong here. This isn't their land and we aren't their people."

"Is that jealousy I detect?" Scouvrel whispered. Almost, I believed he was real. That was exactly something he would say.

"What will Eckelmeyer do?" I pressed, refusing to be drawn in by this madness.

"Last time, he sentenced the adults to death."

"And the children?" I asked, and though my voice was quiet it seemed to echo over the quiet crowd. I expected to see their faces look as shocked as mine, but my breath caught in my throat when I looked at them. They were not silent in shock. They were silent in grim determination.

"Those, he took with him," Olen said.

I leaned over and slapped him across the back of the head. His helmet rang with the blow.

"Olen Chanter, you are such a disgrace!" I let the fury I felt pour into my words. "You should be ashamed of yourself!" I turned to the crowd, jabbing my finger at them to punctuate my words. "You should all be ashamed of yourselves! That's not the kind of people we are!"

Scouvrel hissed excitedly. "Bring him to me, Little Hunter, and I will pay disgrace with disgrace. We could have so much fun teaching him to grovel, you and I."

Stay sane, Allie. Please stay sane.

"But they're Fae lovers!" someone called, and like a dam bursting there were mutters and shouts all around as the crowd came back to life.

Fae lovers! What a silly epitaph. The Fae were cruel and vicious. They'd bargain your life away and they'd nail you to a tree and steal your children – but at least they didn't pretend to be good while they did it.

"You're worse!" I yelled back. "They are evil. But you're choosing evil when you could choose good. Isn't that worse? Aren't you all just that much worse?"

"You need to go now, Allie," Olen said, leaning across the horse to grab the collar of my coat. "Before I have to arrest you, too."

"You're madder than your father," I said, holding his furious gaze through my blindfold, my lower lip trembling.

"Don't make me start to suspect that you sympathize with the Fae, too," he said, shoving me hard so that I fell from the horse into the crowd. "Or I'll have to hang you along with them." He turned to the horses. "Ha!"

He flung my cloak from the heads of the draft horses and slapped their necks, leading them thundering toward his house in the city square. The crowd parted for him, boots kicking me from every direction as they left until I was nothing but a ball of mud and pain, my bow broken, my arrows scattered, only the cage still intact, protected by my curled up body.

I pulled myself painfully from the mud, clutching my aching midsection and watched them go into the center of Skundton. There was a flurry of yelling and then a plume of smoke rose. They'd lit the covered wagon on fire.

"The Court of Mortals is more amusing than I gave it credit for," the Fae in my cage said. "Here I thought you were all dull, but the mortals love pain as much as we do. They torture innocents just as easily. I think they'll welcome the Lady of Cups when she comes in her glory and makes them an offer."

I shivered at her words because she was right. Oh, she was right. And it was breaking my heart.

Maybe it didn't matter if I trapped my sister or not. Maybe the Court of Mortals deserved some of the judgment of the Fae. Maybe, I'd even help them get it.

Chapter Ten

Goodie Chanter was an untidy housekeeper – a fact I was grateful for as I swiped her small mirror from the mantle, tucked it into my cloak and slipped outside and into the woods.

I found a sheltered place in a tangle of willows and drew out the mirror, my hands shaking.

"So vain?" the Lieutenant said from where she sat in her cage chewing on a slice of apple I'd given her.

"Quiet," I hissed.

Did I want to prove I was insane, or prove I wasn't insane? I didn't know, but my heart was pounding like a drum as I huffed over the surface of the cloudy silver mirror and rubbed it with my sleeve.

The moment I lifted it, biting my lip with tension, I saw his face.

"Mirror, mirror, in my hand, who is the fairest in the land?" he said with a smirk.

"Scouvrel?" I whispered.

"Well done. You guessed it with your first try!" He winked.

I fixed him with my darkest look and began to whisper yell. "I don't care how you're doing this. I don't care what magic this is. I don't even care if I'm actually insane, but I have something to say to you!"

"And I have an ear to hear it with, though sadly, only one." His eyes burned as he spoke, as if to remind me of his grisly sacrifice. If he thought that would change my intentions here, he could think again!

"You married me! You tricked me into it."

He laughed. "It was hardly against your will, Little Nightmare. You spoke the words."

"Because you tricked me!"

"I thrive on lies and trickery. You knew that about me." His smile was far too infectious for someone I was furious with.

"What in the world possessed you to do it?"

"Ah Nightmare, you kept looking at me with such marked desire that I saw no way forward except to grant you your darkest desire – me."

I shook my head. Of course, he thought that. In his mind, the whole world was always looking at him with longing.

"And see how that turned out?" I shot back. "I sold you away because I didn't know I possessed you!"

He laughed, a wicked gleam in his eye. "And now that you do know, what would you do with me, Nightmare?"

I wanted to cross my arms over my chest, but I was holding the mirror. I settled for jutting my chin out defiantly.

"Don't try to distract me. Tell me what was in it for you? You know I'll wither and die in seventy years if not more. I have not the charms or glamor of your people. There's no reason to marry me."

"You should know by now, Nightmare, that I give nothing away for free. Not even information. If you want something from me, you will be forced to bargain – and hope that I do not take something dear to you." His eyes twinkled. Was this fun for him?

"You married me without a bargain!" I spat. I stopped, looking around. Had anyone heard? Even in the forest, I had to be careful. "What did I get out of that?"

He looked appalled. "Me, Nightmare. I am your great prize. This is rather like the discoverer of a gold mine objecting to the need to dig. I find it most perplexing. Need I remind you how great a prize I am?"

I pulled the mirror close to my face. "Remind? You'll need to prove it in the first place. You're a horrible, twisted creature and while I've become ... your friend ..." It felt strange to admit that. "I wasn't planning to *marry* you! You took my freedom from me when you married me. I think I at least deserve to know why. That *should* have been part of the bargain!"

"Is it not enough that I wanted you as a permanent ally? A destroyer of worlds, a causer of havoc that even I as the Knave of Courts can respect? Is that not enough?"

"Is that the reason?" I challenged.

"Don't you want to find out?" he asked smoothly, seductively. "Your sister wanted to know. She traded her mortality for Cavariel's answer."

"I would have thought that *immortality* was the thing a person would consider valuable, not *mortality*," I whispered.

"See? You have much to learn from me," Scouvrel said, taunting. "Isn't that worth the price of marrying me? And you have already received my alliance and undying friendship. Your bounty exceeds that of mortal Queens."

"Yes, I'm feeling so fortunate," I said dryly.

"As you should," he agreed, radiating satisfaction.

"But what do you expect from me. You can't mean to ... you can't want to ... you don't expect me to bear your children do you?"

His laugh was cruel. "Fae don't bear children. We steal children. You know that."

"So what is it that you expect from me?" I hissed.

"Everything," he said in a solemn voice that terrified me. "And now, Sweetest of Nightmares, I may not tarry any longer. Thanks to your cruel bargain, I must serve another even crueler than I. And he does not like to be kept waiting." He paused. "Oh, and whatever shiny thing you found to speak to me through, do keep it. I've missed our verbal sparring over these long months. Truth or Lie? You love being my wife."

A look of desperate panic flooded his face before I could answer and then he disappeared from view and the mirror went dark.

"Months?" I asked, but he was already gone.

"Don't you know that the Faewald works differently from the mortal world?" the Lieutenant said, flicking an apple seed out of her cage. "It's been months for him but days for you. Imagine all the fun I've missed while you kept me captive here."

"We're all prisoners," I muttered. "Didn't you hear? I was tricked into marriage."

"And have you finished the game?" she asked disinterestedly.

"Finished what game? You Fae play so many that it's hard to keep up."

She rolled her eyes. "The Marriage game. If you don't finish the game in a year's time, then it will be like you were never married at all."

"And if I do finish the game?" I asked, feeling cold all over.

"Then the marriage can only be ended by death."

"You're so faithful to each other?" I asked, surprised. Most marriages stayed permanent in Skundton. In a town our size there were few options. But even so, some couples lived apart. Some even formalized the arrangement, discarding their former marriages and choosing new lives with other people. It struck me as odd that the Fae didn't do the same.

She snorted. "You misunderstand. If you change your mind later, one of you may end the marriage in death – the death of your partner – with no fear of the Kinslayer coming to rip your beating heart from your chest."

"How lovely," I said dryly. "I can see why you've avoided marriage, Lieutenant."

She sighed. "I suppose you can call me Vhalot since you've been feeding me. It's what I'm known as. I'll keep your secret in exchange for the food. A rare bargain with the Twilight Court."

She sounded resigned.

"My secret?" I asked.

"Anyone who knows you are wed will try to disrupt the union before it can be finalized. It's a game of sorts. A fun way to see if deception and trickery can prevent what you intend before it's complete. It's hard to resist that kind of challenge. It's why most Fae keep an unresolved marriage a secret."

"And if I don't resolve it? What then?" I asked.

She shrugged. "It goes away. If someone disrupted it, you might owe them a prize."

"A prize? What kind of prize?"

"Well, a game isn't fun without a prize. You can usually bargain for what it will be, but it should be something of equal value to your life."

"You're kidding!"

She raised an eyebrow and her lip curled. "Do not mistake me for your precious Knave. I do not joke. I am made to bathe in blood and drink the life of my enemies. I am rippling muscles and biting teeth. I am blade and arrow. I am deadly violence."

I nodded, schooling my expression to neutrality. She was serious. Deadly serious.

"Of course," I agreed. "My mistake."

"Yes. It is."

I felt very guilty for slipping Goodie Chanter's prized possession into my pocket as I gathered up Vhalot's cage, but that didn't stop me from keeping it. Which was crazy, because who purposely invites trouble into their life? And Scouvrel was always trouble. I'd thought our marriage could just go away. That we could just say it was a mistake. Which meant that I hadn't had to think until right now about what it might mean to be married to one of the Fae. About what might be expected. About what might be forced on me.

I shivered, suddenly cold to the core.

Chapter Eleven

I waited until nightfall because that's when you do bad things – or at least things other people might think of as bad.

If I was being honest with myself, I wasn't sure if I could really harm someone from my town – a human with a family and friends who were likely also my family and friends – but at the same time, I was certainly angry enough to want to.

I hadn't been able to repair my bow – not after the way it had been cracked – and building a new one took time. Which was why I had my hunting knife strapped to my leg and the old bow I'd found on the paths. I'd had to restring it and I wasn't confident in the draw with how weathered it looked, but I hoped it was good enough to be painful if I shot someone at close range. And that was going to have to do.

I stashed a parcel of food – as much as I could take without my mother or Goodie Chanter noticing – and a pile of blankets I'd pilfered from laundry lines around town. Okay, so it wasn't a very honest thing to do. I wasn't feeling all that honest right now. It was all rolled up in a hollow log just west of the town because if I managed this, then that's where I was going to take these people – west, over that winding, twisting mountain trail to that half-ruined cart and through the oak tree. It was my only chance to get them out of here. And I wasn't going to watch some pompous knight with inflexible rules execute people just for being linked to the Fae in people's minds. Not while I was here, at any rate.

"Why go to so much trouble for those not of your Court, Mortal?" Vhalot had asked me.

"Because right is right," I said as I made preparations.

"Those others in your town don't agree," she'd said with an edge to her voice. "And I've been watching you. You steal and lie. You take and choose. You are no better than they are and no better than we are."

"That's your opinion," I'd spat.

"What if we only judge you by your own conscience? By your own morality?" she'd asked, still calm despite my rising emotions. "Would you even be able to stand up to that much scrutiny?"

I ignored the question. I didn't like being reminded that I wasn't living up to even my own idea of what was right or wrong. But this – this one thing could help. Couldn't it?

"I'm going to leave you here," I'd said before I left her stashed in the eagle nest tree. I put a cloth over her cage to keep the birds away. "Where I'm going, arrows might fly, and I don't want you damaged in the crossfire."

"I mistrust altruism," she said, muffled through the fabric.

"Distrust all you like. I'm doing this for you."

"Then let me return the favor. There are four things you must do to complete the marriage game. The first is to take his hand in return – in any way, it matters not. If you haven't done that, then you haven't even started the game."

"Thanks," I'd muttered. But my heart was already sinking. I could remember – clear as river water – how I'd taken Scouvrel's hand and kissed it right before he'd pushed me through the stone circle. No wonder he'd looked so surprised.

It was all I could do not to pull the mirror out of my pocket and look for him again before I left. Which was crazy, because he'd probably trap me into doing whatever this second thing was. Caring about what he thought was like a moth caring about the flame. Stupid and dangerous.

I pushed the urge aside and steeled my nerves for what was coming.

The night guards were sloppy. Sneaking into town through the shadows outside the light of their watch-fires was laughably easy. If this town was the same as the one I'd left, then people probably did it all the time to sneak off into the woods and meet up with lovers or friends. Even if you didn't take the roads, there were enough small gaps between houses and fences to move with ease into the town.

And now here I was outside the barracks or jail or whatever that was next to Olen's house. I slid through the shadows with my back to the rough stone of the wall of his house. Heldra's voice filtered down from the open window.

"If there's any chance that they know how to get into the stone circle, Olen, then we have to take it," she was saying.

"I have my orders, Heldra."

"Psssh!" She sounded agitated. "Your orders! I'm talking about our *son*!"

"I won't violate them. Sir Eckelmeyer has put his trust in me."

And now she sounded desperate. "Olen Chanter! Fae take you if you don't use what little power you have to bring our boy back!"

I'd never heard Heldra so upset. I shivered at her words. Mostly, because I'd be feeling the exact same way as she was if that was my little boy in the Faewald. If there was one person I never expected to agree with, it was Heldra Thatcher.

"If I'd wanted to marry a crazy woman, Heldra, I would have married Allie Hunter. Now, leave me be. I have a letter to write to Sir Eckelmeyer." His voice was cold.

"You jest with me, Olen. And I am in no mood for jesting." There were tears on the edges of her words.

"Neither am I. Which of us is the Knight here, Heldra?"

I rolled my eyes. If he'd talked like that to me, he'd be quickly finding a new place to sleep. Maybe he had made the right decision on who to marry.

Married! And to a tangled Fae! I needed to figure out what to do about that ... but not now. I shook my head to clear it. I hadn't been wrong to bargain his service away. I really hadn't. It was his own fault for marrying me without telling me.

Focus, Allie! Focus!

"I hate you, Olen!" Heldra spat. "I hate you for not caring. But I won't leave you, because I have two other babies who need me and fool that I was, you're their father. But if you lose just one more of them, I will pry that sword from your hand and take that knighthood from you so fast you'll wonder how you lived as long as you did."

Olen sighed and then the door slammed, and I ran from the pool of shadows under the window to the pool surrounding the door of the barracks. I fumbled at the door latch in the darkness, trying to slip in before Heldra came out in the yard. It was locked. I drew my knife to see if I could ease the latch, but Heldra ran down the steps to her house, the moonlight shining off her hood.

I ducked back into the shadows, pressed against the edge of the door and hoping she wouldn't see me.

Her head shot up, looking right at my shadowy hiding place.

Uh oh.

She stalked to the barracks door. Something shone in her hand.

The key.

Did I have the guts to knock Heldra on the head and take it? I'd never liked Heldra. And yet I wasn't sure I could be violent to her. Especially not now. Not with her living the life I only narrowly escaped – a life I was now realizing would have been stifling and painfully disappointing.

She reached the door, slotting the key into the lock. The moment of truth.

Before I could raise a hand, she noticed me in the shadows. Her eyes went wide and then she held up a hand as if to stop me and looked furtively over my shoulder.

"Are you going to open the circle and get my boy back?" she hissed, eyebrows drawing together.

Wait. She wasn't going to scream? Wasn't going to attack me?

"I'm trying to," I whispered.

"Try harder." Her whisper was desperate. "And take the key with you or it will look bad for me."

She spun on her heel and strode toward the little gate that led out to the street.

I let out a long breath and turned the key in the lock, slipping it free and opening the door. Who would have ever thought that Heldra Thatcher would help me rescue a family of Travelers? The world really had turned upside down.

I found them huddled sadly around a tiny fire in the barracks grate. Dozens of orderly beds lay in long rows on either side of the fireplace, but the Traveler family was on none of them, choosing instead to sleep on shoulders and laps as they cried softly together around the fire.

A jagged splinter of sympathy stabbed my heart.

Curses on Olen and his stupid Sir Eckelmeyer!

And curses on the whole town of Skundton.

They were no better than Werex or Cavariel. No better than my dear husband Scouvrel and his horrible tricks. They were just way worse at what they did. They were like a toddler smashing flowers for the fun of destruction. And this poor family was the flowers.

"Shhh," I whispered when the woman looked up at me. "We need to slip out before anyone notices that I'm here."

"The cart," she began but I cut her off with a gesture.

"Is gone. Take only what you can carry. I have blankets stashed in a tree if we can get that far."

She nodded, the man nodding, too. Carefully, they shook small sleepy-eyed children awake. They were three boys – none older than seven or younger than three and their owlish brown eyes melted my heart.

"Come on, little hunters," I whispered. "We need to sneak together. Can you stay quiet?"

Three big-eyed nods.

"Who are you?" the littlest one asked.

"I'm a Nightmare to your enemies," I whispered back with a wink. "And a friend to you."

His smile was quicksilver.

I grinned, trying to look confident for them. "Now, follow me, little hunters, and keep your footstep quiet!"

I slipped out the door, leading the little ones through the night, their parents slipping into line behind me. Olen had not set a guard on their barracks. He'd trusted the key and he'd trusted his wife and the town. He'd probably even trusted me. But I didn't feel guilty about that. Not when he'd imprisoned innocents.

As we reached the edge of the west road a horse whickered nearby and the littlest boy called out, "Meadow!"

His mother fell to her knees, wrapping her hand around his mouth, her eyes brimming with fear. At the same moment, one of the guards at the village edge spoke.

"What was that?"

He lifted up a torch, walking toward us.

"Head west past the treeline and wait for me there," I whispered before I tugged down my blindfold and walked through the shadows toward the guard. It was easier to see at night with only my spirit vision.

"It's only me," I said loudly, drawing attention to where I was so that the Travelers could slip out into the forest.

"Hunter?" one of the guards asked, holding his torch higher.

I took a bold step into the light of his torch and froze. With my spirit sight, he flickered slightly. That was normal.

But what wasn't normal was how the very edges of him seemed to be unraveling and tangling back together again.

Just like the Fae.

Chapter Twelve

My heart leapt in my throat as he drew his sword. The other guard stepped out from behind him with a crossbow raised, aimed at me.

Well, you have their attention, Allie. What now? Could I really harm ... or kill? ... people from Skundton? But I didn't recognize these two. They weren't men I grew up with. Did that make a difference? They're still men, Allie. They have mothers and fathers, maybe even wives and children. Could you hurt them? Does that make you any better than Hulanna?

I swallowed.

The other guard was fraying at the edges, too. What did that mean? Did it mean that they weren't really human anymore? I could hurt or kill someone who wasn't really human. I could do that.

I paused.

What was I thinking? Was I really making someone seem inhuman to myself so I could hurt him? I was no better than the Fae. None of us were. What were we going to do?

I shook myself and stepped forward.

"Of course, it's me," I said scornfully. "Who did you think it was?"

"Who's to say?" the guard with the crossbow said warily. "Sir Chanter ordered us to enforce curfew. And you are not in your home. Maybe you aren't even you. They say the creatures from on top of the mountain can change their faces."

"The Fae?" I asked, and he flinched. Interesting. That wasn't a legend I'd heard, unless he meant glamor. I let a little scorn into my tone. "They can make themselves appear gloriously beautiful. Would you say that *I* look gloriously beautiful?"

"No," the guard with the sword said, flushing a little. "Sorry, miss, but no."

"I didn't think so." I took another two steps, pretending that I wasn't worried about the crossbow bolt making wobbling circles in the trembling hands of its owner.

At the edge of the treeline, I heard a stick snap. The guard with the crossbow started to turn and I stepped smartly forward and plucked the crossbow from his hand. His finger slipped on the trigger and the bolt shot wildly into the night, pinging when it hit the weathervane on a nearby house.

"If you want to guard against Fae, you'll need to be a lot sharper than this," I said firmly. "You don't even know how to hold your crossbow straight, much less hit a target. I was a single pace from you, and you missed me!"

Forceful and confident, Allie. Make them think you're in charge. That's how Scouvrel did it.

"But I – " the guard began and I heard another snap in the forest so I raised my voice to cut him off.

"And you! The one with the sword. You just stood there like a fool! What do you two think you're playing at? When the Fae pour through the stone circle and ride down the hills on unicorns, hacking and slashing with their bronze swords or fluttering down from the sky on wings of smoke will you be hitting weathercocks with your crossbow bolts and holding up torches gaping, or will you be able to actually raise an alarm and alert this town of danger?"

"I – "

I rode right over his protest. "What's your signal? Is it the bell over there on the post? Why did neither of you ring it?"

"We're the guards here, not you," the guard with the sword said, finally recovering himself. There were sounds of arguing in the nearby house as the residents debated whether to go out and check on their weathercock.

"Yes," I said, moving in close the way I knew Scouvrel would if he were here and smiling his very same cruel smile. "And because I'm not here guarding this town, you'd better do it right. Because whether people admit it or not, I'm still Hunter here and if you don't keep my people safe, I'll hunt you down and make you pay for your negligence."

"No, you won't," a calm voice said from behind me. I spun to see Olen standing there, a grim look on his face and his lantern held high. He was a full head taller than I was. But in my spirit vision, he was still the hunched, nervous boy he'd been when I'd known him before. He wavered a little as he spoke. "There is no Hunter here, Allie."

"Then train your guards to actually defend this town," I said, shoving the crossbow at his chest. "And I won't need to be Hunter."

Fear made my knees tremble. There was a whole town of them here and only one of me. And yet, I just kept seeing those innocent brown eyes in my mind – the eyes of the little children my former friend had imprisoned. The little hunters waiting for me in the woods. I needed to buy them time.

Olen grabbed my wrist, taking the crossbow and tossing it to the guard who had lost it. The guard guttered like a dying flame in my vision, his edges tangling up even more as the moments passed. Olen's eyes never left mine and in my spirit vision, they seemed to be filled with flame.

"They're doing their jobs. They're not the ones here making a disturbance. You are. Go home, Allie."

I knew when to keep my mouth shut – and that was right now when he was giving me exactly what I needed – permission to go down that road and back into the woods to help the Travelers. I kept my lips pressed tightly together.

Olen dragged me in close, his grip still painfully tight on my wrist.

"And Allie, I hope for your sake that you had nothing to do with what I just found in the barracks."

"What did you find?" I asked innocently and his eyes narrowed.

"Nothing. I found *nothing*."

I tried to feign confusion and defiance – like how I would be if I hadn't made those barracks empty and didn't know what he was talking about.

"Then I guess you have no reason to be upset with me."

He pressed his lips together angrily, his spirit flaring brightly for a moment before dulling again, and then he shoved me away. "Just go. And if I or my guards find you breaking curfew again, it will be *you* locked up in the barracks."

It was all I could do to keep my mouth shut but I did it. I kept it shut while my mind fed me one smart response after another after another. If only Scouvrel was here. He would say them all and then wipe that smarmy look right off Olen's face. But I didn't dare do it.

And I needed to stop wishing that my Faerie husband were here. I was making my own heart too complicated with all these emotions. Emotions were like fish coated in lard. They slipped from your hands and took off down the stream before you could gasp for breath.

Not safe, Allie. Feed it to your inner fire and be done with it.

I strode confidently out of town, forcing myself not to look back until the shadows hid me completely. Even then, when I finally stole a glance over my shoulder, Olen was still there in the pool of firelight staring after me up the dark road. I swallowed hard, pulled my blindfold back up, and hoped I could be quiet enough as I searched for the Travelers and hoped even harder that he didn't really believe I'd rescued them – at least not until I got them to safety.

Chapter Thirteen

When I returned home, I was really going to be in trouble. Olen would know by then that it was me who had stolen the Travelers – wouldn't he? And I couldn't seem to care. Not when my legs and arms were so tired that they felt like they were going to drop off – and I was only carrying the littlest of the children, his sweet dark curly-haired head resting on my shoulder and his little back bowed out as if he were actually comfortable with his legs wrapped around my waist and my arms wrapped around his back.

I had never seen myself as a possible mother for children, but holding this little boy made something melt inside me. It also brought up questions. What would a real marriage to Scouvrel mean? Beyond just the fact that I'd be married to a citizen of hell – a terrible twisted creature I'd learned to call friend, well, it would mean no children. Ever.

I held the axe handle torch up with one of the hands gripping him – its spiritual flame harmless to him. It lit my path enough that I could lead them all over the rocky ground as silently as we could manage in the dark of night.

Behind me, the two Traveler adults huffed and grunted in near silence. We hadn't said a word since I found them huddling in the woods together. Not even when I drew out the blankets and food and we wrapped up the children in the warmth of the blankets and bound the supplies into bundles the parents could carry.

There had been murmured whispers when the first of the children stumbled, so overcome by exhaustion that he'd tripped and begun to cry. Once his mother calmed him, we'd returned to silence, but now with the children in our arms.

Luckily, the spirit torch seemed to keep the ghouls back, and while I could hear their longing howls in the night, they didn't come near the bright glow.

Someone needed to do something about them. In all my time as a child, they'd never been so out of control. If Knights had replaced Hunters, then the Knights had better get on that. A community couldn't survive with wild ghouls flooding its borders. They might not hurt full-grown people, but they'd snatch children given half a chance. And they sometimes lured the elderly to their deaths, too.

The thought sent a stab of real fear through my heart. Because if tonight had taught me anything it was that Olen couldn't be trusted to protect my town. And neither could his men. Which meant there was only me. And while I'd been plotting to trap my sister, I hadn't made a good enough arrangement for the innocents of Skundton. Or for my parents.

And I hadn't found a way to rescue the mortal children from the Fae realm. Frustration and fire filled my steps. There wasn't enough time. And there wasn't enough Allie. But neither of those things was a good enough excuse. I'd spent days running all over the countryside looking for weapons when I should have been planning and organizing. I'd gone about this all wrong.

I'd been thinking like a teenage girl and a stalker of prey instead of like one of the Fae or like my sister and if I couldn't learn to think like them, if I couldn't learn to be smarter and deeper than I was right now, then everyone was going to suffer. Maybe the adults of Skundton deserved that after what they'd almost done to these Travelers. But the children didn't deserve it.

Each time I looked back at the Traveler parents, I saw the fear and desperation in their eyes. I didn't dare stop to tell them I had a plan, that if we could just get to the wagon, they would be completely safe. Mostly because I didn't dare stop long enough to be caught. Who knew when Olen would realize it really had been me who freed them? Who knew when he'd send men not burdened with exhausted children to chase after us? Or even chase us himself on horseback? Though a horse would not get far on this narrow path.

And what kind of fool named his horse Blossom? Seriously? Not Charger, or Sparkhoof, or Lightning, or something fitting to your first warhorse but ... Blossom? Olen was the worst knight.

Unless he'd let me go because he wanted me to help the Travelers.

But that didn't make sense, did it?

I glanced back again and tried to give the Traveler's a hopeful look, but their anxious eyes only spurred me forward. This part of the climb was the hardest. Especially now, in the dark. And I didn't dare light anything on fire to help us find the way. If anyone saw the light and followed it here, then they might find the ruined wagon. And if they found that wagon none of these Travelers would be safe.

My mind was wandering. I needed to focus. I needed to think of a way to save all the children – the Traveler children like the sweet boy sleeping in my arms, the stolen children, the town children. They didn't deserve what was coming for them. None of them did. And while I might be giving up on that town, I wasn't going to give up on them. I just couldn't. I had to fight. I had to win.

It seemed to take far too long as my arms grew heavier and heavier, but eventually, the ruined wagon came into sight and I slumped to my knees in relief.

"Are you too tired to go on?" the woman Traveler asked, squatting beside me, her son yawning in her arms. Her eyes were huge by the light of the torch and she glowed slightly silver.

I could see the wagon shimmering in my spirit sight. It looked magical in the light of the torch.

"We're here," I whispered. "There's a door in that wagon that will take you to safety – to other Travelers. One of them called herself the Loremistress."

"Then we should hurry," her husband said, nodding but tight in his every movement. I wasn't the only one feeling anxious.

I stood, my weary legs protesting every movement, and stumbled across the loose stone to the wagon, every step a struggle.

Hang in there, Allie.

We were almost there.

There was a shout from the hill behind me and I quickened my pace.

"How could we have been seen?" the Traveler man asked roughly. "It's the middle of the night!"

"I don't know," his wife said, but her words were muffled as she stepped into the wagon. "There's nothing in here."

"Keep walking," I whispered. "The door is hidden."

Her husband waited for me to go first, so I hurried in after her, stumbling and barely catching myself as my feet hit the ground on the other side of the door and I found myself in a ring of surprised Travelers around the oak tree. Their campfire danced merrily – twice as high as I was – and a fiddle stopped playing only moments after I emerged. People froze, breathless and flushed, hands clasped together as if we had surprised a dance. Which we had.

"It's true," the Traveler man gasped, stumbling into the circle of Travelers from behind me, relief and hope softening his face. "I didn't dare hope it was."

"Arvi? Is that you?" one of the shocked men around the fire called, standing up in surprise.

The Loremistress strode out from the crowd and took the sleeping child from my arms with authority. "Sister, brother, we have places for you here. Let us settle your children."

I sagged in relief.

"Thank you," the woman I'd saved said, kissing my cheek before handing her other boy over to a motherly looking Traveler with a warm smile and lined face.

"I need to go back right away," I said awkwardly. "Those voices on the hill – I need them to find me, so they don't find the wagon."

The woman I'd saved grabbed my sleeve. "What is the name of the one who saved us?"

"I'm Allie Hunter," I said. I felt uncomfortable in the middle of all this attention. They were all so happy. So whole. They didn't fit in my world of brokenness and desperation.

"There's a bow and a blade hidden near your town, Allie. And a stick. This is known to us all and I offer it as a gift of thanks for what you've done tonight," the woman whispered to me. "The stick is a torch that will make you invisible to the Fae." She glanced at the handle in my hand. "Though perhaps you already know that. The blade will slice through worlds. The bow will pierce only wicked hearts. Find them and you will have all that you need to defend the innocent as darkness flows over the earth."

She ducked her head and hurried away before I could thank her, but the Loremistress leaned in, the little boy still in her arms. "You saved those whose names you do not know from a fate you did not guess. We remember those who remember us. I doubt you'll come to us looking for anything for yourself, but if you bring others who need help here, we will help them for your sake. Remember this."

I nodded.

"And remember that blood is blood."

Which sounded like crazy talk, but I was far too tired to argue. I stumbled back through the oak tree, spirit torch held high, and tried to get as much distance between myself and the wagon as I could before whoever was calling in the woods found me. I'd do whatever it took to keep those people safe. Even if it meant breaking my neck in the dark.

And as I stumbled and fell and hurried through the dark, I kept thinking of the rusty blade I'd hidden in the tree. Could it be the blade that cut through worlds? Could I use it to cut into the Faewald?

It was time to stop being a trusting girl and start being a hunting woman. I was beginning to hatch a plan to save the children. All the children. And I was going to see it through one way or another. But first, I needed to gather up my things and talk to my mother.

I could almost see Scouvrel's dark eyes winking at me as I ran.

Chapter Fourteen

My legs were so far past aching that they were just one long unending scream of pain as I stumbled through the darkness with my spirit torch held up.

I still didn't know if I'd made the right choice to choose to run through the night with my second sight instead of my normal sight, but I didn't dare light a real torch, and at least the spirit torch made everything brighter and clearer even if it failed to show me tripping hazards or some of the trees.

A pair of silvery hinds – Faerie creatures – had leapt up from a nearby thicket when I passed, the spirit light visible enough to them that they scrambled to be free of it. The same had happened with a swarm of those magenta flying creatures – I'd decided to name them Pink Furies until I knew what they were really called – and they'd tumbled all over themselves to get away. Maybe I could single-handedly deal with the ghoul problem with this – if I had time.

I slipped the mirror out of my pocket. I'd kept telling myself I wasn't going to do it, but as the journey wore on, I was losing willpower.

Scouvrel's surprised eye filled the mirror. It looked the same, spirit vision or real vision. Interesting.

"Husband," I whispered.

His laugh made my spine tingle. "Nightmare. Pleasure at seeing my face?"

He looked rumpled like he was rising from sleep.

"Four," I said. There was no way I'd say anything more. His grin was already too large. "My time is short. Will my sister invade soon?"

He shrugged. "Who can say? It's been a week for me since we spoke. How long has it been for you?"

"Not a full day," I whispered. I stumbled over a stick and flinched at the sharp sound it made. I couldn't keep this conversation up for long. "If you can't tell me that, tell me where the mortal children are hidden. Are they scattered all over the Faewald?"

His eyebrow rose and he hesitated.

"Must I bargain with you?" I said through gritted teeth.

"I still owe you for our last kiss," he said with a grin. "The mortal children are hidden in the Court of Silk and the Court of Cups. Pursue them at your own peril."

"Thank you," I breathed, and his eyebrows shot up in surprise.

I jammed the mirror back in my pocket. I needed to hurry.

I stumbled over a log as if to punctuate my thoughts, biting my tongue on the way down and skinning my knuckles. It was a good reminder that spirit sight was not real sight. I was so close to the Chanters' house. If I could just make it there and grab that sword, I could carry on my mission.

My original plan had been to find what Hulanna wanted – humanity. Then find what tools I could to stop her – this trove of Traveler magic items. Then find a way to make her nervous.

I didn't care as much about that now, though it would still be useful. What I needed to do now was save those mortal children, while I still could, before that opportunity also slipped between my fingers.

My pursuers were getting closer, too. And I didn't recognize any of their voices. I'd led them on a merry chase through the woods, but now it was time to lose them.

"I heard a crash up there," one of them said from far, far too close behind me. His voice was raspy.

"Whoever it is, we've almost got him cornered," another voice said. "Probably just a farmer with a still in the woods, but Sir Eckelmeyer likes to know who doesn't know how to keep curfew in a community."

"So do I," the raspy voice said.

I could see the house lights flickering up ahead in the strange half-there way that things did with my second sight. I was so close. I eased up and slipped through the shadows, trying to keep myself from running. I'd only attract more notice if I did. I slipped again, hitting a bush, the branches scraping my skin and making a loud rustling sound.

I could hear feet pounding on the forest floor. They'd be on me in a moment. They were that close.

I forced my breath to come evenly. Think, Allie, think!

These men worked for Eckelmeyer. They wanted to capture me. That meant they'd take anything I had on me. I couldn't afford to lose these things. Carefully, I hid the axe handle and my bow and arrows in the bushes, grabbing the key from my pocket and shoving it in the dead grass beside it. I could find this place again. I could.

I just needed to be sure they didn't search it.

I took a deep breath, pulled up my blindfold and sprinted into the night. If I was far enough from the bushes when they caught me, they wouldn't search them.

Someone grunted from right behind me and then my legs were knocked out from under me and I fell, sprawling, to the forest floor. A moment later a heavy weight was on my back.

"Just a girl," the raspy voice said. "Where were you off to, love? Trysting? You're young to be up to that kind of trouble. You won't want whelps until you've got a good man to tend you. A soldier, maybe. That's a steady paycheck."

"With so much charm it's a wonder you're not already married," I let my disgust leak into my tone.

"Who says I'm not, love?"

"Who says, *I'm* not?" I countered. "My husband is the most evil and terrifying thing you could ever meet. He could kill you with a sewing pin before you could draw your blade."

He laughed. "I don't believe you."

I laughed, too, but my laugh sounded insane in my own ears, even though every word I'd said was true.

"We're taking too long," the other voice said. "They'll send another scout team to look for us if we don't meet at the rendezvous. Haul her up and drag her with us."

Rough hands pulled the collar of my jacket until I stood. The soldier forced my hands behind my back, binding them with harsh twine that bit hard into my flesh.

It was too dark to see faces but the smell of garlic and stale wine was strong on raspy-voice. These were the men in the employ of the great Sir Eckelmeyer, were they? This was the company Olen was mixing with? He was going to regret having such allies.

It was all I could do not to look longingly at the lit window and my mother's silhouette inside. In a few hours, when dawn lit the sky, she'd be getting worried. And I needed to warn her. It was going to be up to her to get the children out of this town.

"Walk faster, girl. We don't have all night."

"Seems like you had all night when you spent it bumbling through the woods like two bears just risen from hibernation," I muttered.

"What's that?"

"Just ignore her," the other voice said.

We marched in silence as I thought through the options I had. Maybe Sir Eckelmeyer would be a reasonable sort – though his men didn't seem reasonable and people tended to attract others like themselves.

"This Sir Eckelmeyer, he's a fair man?" I asked.

"Your town is under curfew by order of Sir Olen Chanter. That makes you a lawbreaker," one of the men said.

A worrying response. No comment on whether he was fair, only that I was already guilty in their minds.

Maybe, Sir Eckelmeyer would be too busy worrying about the Fae to bother about a girl found wandering in the woods. After all, no one could prove I'd done anything wrong – except Heldra. And somehow, I didn't think she was going to say anything. She'd be in as much trouble as I was if she did. I'd thrown her key into the woods just like she'd asked. No one could prove she'd taken it – or who had freed those Travelers. As long as we were both quiet about it, we should be safe.

"I suppose you'll all be very busy guarding us against the Fae," I suggested.

"What do you know about Fae?" the one shoving me forward asked.

"Enough to know it will take more than a few bullies skulking in the woods to stop them."

"We're the Band of the White Hood," the other man said. "We don't skulk. We are not bullies. We are the personal armsmen of Sir Eckelmeyer the Glorious."

"That's his name? 'The Glorious'?"

"It's his title."

"That's very handy. I'd like my name to tell people what to think, too. Maybe I'll call myself, 'Allie Hunter the Beautiful and Very Rich.' Ooof!"

Something had struck me in the back of the head. I bit my tongue and tasted blood. These fellows didn't like sarcasm or mocking. I might have been given a long leash by Olen, but it looked like I'd lost that freedom.

I was cursing in my mind.

I'd missed my chance to cut my way back into the Faewald, or to find some way to win my people back. But I didn't regret freeing the Travelers tonight. And I didn't regret collecting the artifacts – not entirely. Especially now that I knew they could actually help me. I just wished I'd had more time.

Snow began to fall, thick and white as we reached the guard post on the edge of the town. The guards I'd seen last night were nowhere to be seen now. In their place, long lines of snorting horses and men in armor stood, watching their breath cloud the air and their feet churn up the road.

Their armor glinted in the starlight, and clinked in the breeze as chainmail brushed against plate and scabbards against chain.

I felt like someone had put a rock in my belly. There were hundreds of men in armor. No women at all. They all wore white hoods, easy to see in the light of their torches. And they wore matching grim expressions. There would be no compassion here. There would be no hope for anyone who stepped in their path.

More than ever, I wondered if it might not be the worst thing for Hulanna to march through the circle and level them all.

"Found something in your sweep, Corne?" one of the men on the horses asked. There was a fancy clump of red feathers flowing from the back of his helm. An officer, I supposed.

"Yes, Master at Arms!" Corne– the one with the garlic breath – said almost crisply. "We found this miscreant wandering in the woods in the middle of the night."

"Nice work, Corne. Bring her straight to the guardhouse. By order of Sir Eckelmeyer, all persons found breaking curfew are to be presumed to be spies, detained, and questioned."

That didn't sound good.

Chapter Fifteen

Sir Eckelmeyer and his men must have arrived shortly after I fled with the Travelers. That was the only explanation I could think of for why he looked so at ease in Olen and Heldra's house.

They dragged me up the steps and into the stone house with a lot more energy than required and threw me to the floor.

At least Heldra kept a clean house. This floor had been scrubbed well and recently. It's always nice to do your bleeding and dying on a clean floor.

"What's this?"

I heard the voice before I could look up and see the man. Black boots and a white tabard – the edge of it stained by mud and travel dust – filled my vision. I struggled to my knees, my bound hands behind my back making it more difficult than it should have been.

Olen's face – green and sickly – was the first thing I saw from behind the looming figure of Sir Eckelmeyer. He must not like seeing me treated this way. Well, wasn't that nice?

Heldra's dining room table had been stripped and laid out with what must be her best tablecloth and stacks of ledgers and scrolls. The chairs had all been arranged on the side farthest from me. That was where Olen was sitting, looking like he'd just swallowed a slug. Behind him, the door that must lead to his family's private rooms was cracked slightly open and I saw one wide eye staring out at me. Heldra.

And beside the door was a framed silver mirror. I felt a wave of nausea wash over me at the sight of the mirror. If Scouvrel took this moment to look at me, he might be too much of a distraction in this thorny circumstance.

I tore my eyes away from Heldra's anxious gaze, avoiding the mirror. At least with the blindfold up, no one could tell where I was looking to give her away.

"A dirty girl with a blindfold over her eyes?" the voice asked. It was far too quiet of a voice. I felt the hair stand up on the back of my neck and arms. I didn't like that voice.

When I'd heard the name "Sir Eckelmeyer" I'd envisioned a portly man a little older than my father with wide shoulders and a thick mustache. In my mind, his voice was baritone.

The real Sir Eckelmeyer was none of those things. For starters, he was barely older than Olen. Maybe he was even a year or two younger. His face was hairless without even the stubble of a beard trying to grow back. His hair – light in color – was cut so short that I wasn't sure how they got the shears that close to his head. And while his expression was grim and his eyes were flat, his narrow face was not ugly. If he smiled, if he hadn't been dressed in steel and a white tabard, I might have mistaken him for a new villager. Maybe even that squire Olen was going to offer me to in marriage.

That squire had better not be Corne. I shuddered at the thought.

"We found her in the woods after dark when we were scouting," Corne said. I could hear the pleasure he found in delivering me up as a prisoner. I had a feeling he was the type who would tell lies about his old grandmother and offer her to the executioner if he thought it would improve his reputation with the Knights.

"Near the circle?" Eckelmeyer said sharply.

"On the mountains west of here."

"And what were you doing there, girl?" Eckelmeyer said quietly. "Standing watch for your Faerie allies?"

"I was picking berries," I lied.

"At night?"

I tried to gesture to my blindfold, forgetting that my hands were tied behind my back and settled for a one-armed shrug. "Night or day, both are the same when you're blind."

Not entirely true, but how was he to know that?

Olen shuffled uncomfortably in his chair.

"Interesting. And where are the berries?"

"I dropped them when I was chased by shadows," I said, trying to sound as if I had been frightened. "How was I to know they were the emissaries of a great Lord?"

"Knight."

"Pardon me?"

"I am a Knight, not a Lord, girl," Eckelmeyer said sharply. "Do you know this child, Sir Chanter?"

He turned to Olen who looked uncomfortable.

My cheeks were growing hot. Child? I might be older than he was! Sort of.

"She is the one I wrote to you about, Sir Eckelmeyer," Olen said, bending his head slightly out of respect. Had he always had such terrible judgment about people? Well, he'd married Heldra. That should have made his inability to judge people pretty obvious. "I'd hoped you would bring a squire to wed her."

The mirror behind him remained empty. Where was Scouvrel?

"Stand up, girl." Eckelmeyer's tone held interest. Uh oh. My heart seemed to freeze. The mouse didn't like the regard of the snake – and neither did I.

But I had to remember, I was no mouse. I was the killer of mice.

I stood with as much grace as I could manage.

Eckelmeyer made an exasperated sound in his throat. "Cut her free."

I was tugged a step backward and then my hands were free. I snatched them forward, gently rubbing the scored flesh.

"She's not that young, I suppose," Eckelmeyer said as if he were judging livestock.

He rose and rounded the table. It was all I could do not to flinch when he took my chin between two fingers, tilting my head one way and then the other. His breath smelled of mint leaves. "She might even be passable if she were well-scrubbed. And if she didn't wear such a sour expression."

My hands balled into fists. I did not care if he thought I was the ugliest hag ever to have lived. In fact, I might prefer that. His judgment – his opinions – were nothing to me. But now was not the time to say that, Allie. Not the time to get yourself locked up or your throat cut.

I bit my tongue to keep it still.

"Do you think you might have a squire who could wed her, Sir Eckelmeyer?" Olen asked diffidently. "That would certainly solve one of my problems here. She has too much energy to live as a meek daughter, and the men here her age were minded by her as children. It won't do to marry her to them, and yet we need a channel for all that excess energy."

"Hmmm," Eckelmeyer said. "Do you have skills, girl?"

"I can hold my tongue," I said, more as a reminder to myself than as an actual list of my skills.

"That remains to be seen," Eckelmeyer countered.

"All the girls of our village are raised to cookery, weaving, gardening, sewing, knitting, wool gathering, herding, cleaning, cheesemaking, and the other womanly arts," Olen offered helpfully.

Except I was no more than barely passable at those things. I had been raised to hunt and trap anything that could move. But I was no fool. I was a rabbit in the mouth of a dog right now. If I remained very still, I might yet find a chance to flee when the dog grew distracted. If I fought too hard now, he would bite down and sever my spine.

The sly smile on Eckelmeyer's face was making it hard not to sweat right through my clothing. I swallowed and his smile grew by a hair.

"I think it would be best to keep this one close. That way I can determine if she was up to any kind of misadventure in the forest tonight or if she is conspiring with our enemies as Corne fears. It will also help with your concern, Sir Chanter, for I have been myself searching for a suitable wife and who knows, perhaps I could see past her blindness and plain face and bless her with my troth."

I was going to 'bless' him with my foot in his belly if he didn't stop this nonsense.

The mirror on the wall flickered. "What's this, Nightmare?"

So now he turned up! I clenched my eyes shut and willed him to silence. What if the others heard him?

Olen cleared his throat uncomfortably.

"You object?" Eckelemeyer asked, and the glint of satisfaction explained everything to me. Somehow, he knew that Olen and I had once been friends. Somehow, he knew that Olen still had a small soft spot for me. And he was going to use that against us both.

"What are these mortal mice plotting, Little Nightmare? Are these your enemies? I could take their heads as trophies and hang them over my bath. Would that please you? Would it show you how *valuable* I am as a husband?"

I didn't dare answer him.

"Of course not, Sir Eckelmeyer," Olen stumbled over his words in his haste to respond. "Any woman would be honored to be your wife, though I'm sure your prospects are far higher than village girls."

"Wife! This is my challenger for your affections?" Scouvrel hooted. "I will remember the back of that head and search for it when next I enter the mortal world. This man shall pay for his presumption. I bear no challenge well."

As if I didn't know that. After all, hadn't I seen him kill two other Fae to have the inside of my cage to himself?

"Humility is a trait every Knight should embrace," Eckelmeyer said, impervious to the threats being leveled against him. I didn't know if he meant that for himself or for Olen. "Go clean up, girl. I will see you back here for dinner tonight. And wear clothing that befits a woman of marriageable age rather than these farm boy rags."

I heard Scouvrel hiss in the background.

I nodded, not trusting my voice – or my good luck. If I was fast, I could be well on my way to the Faewald before they caught me again.

Chapter Sixteen

Well, this was a fine mess. I couldn't imagine a worse choice to lead the Court of Mortals here in Skundton than Sir Eckelmeyer. Worse, Scouvrel knew about him now, which meant the Faewald knew about him. And I didn't like showing them our weaknesses.

Sir Eckelmeyer was going to be very surprised when he found out to whom I was married – and how dangerous that might be to him. I had a feeling that the Knave of Courts could cause a lot of chaos for a pompous stick-in-the-mud like Eckelmeyer. That might be one benefit to being married to the Knave.

Married! I still hadn't made my peace with that. I hadn't intended to marry. Certainly not to a Fae. Certainly not to Scouvrel who twisted me up in knots and made my head spin. He wasn't safe. He wasn't tame. I had no idea what to do about him now.

I was shivering so hard that my teeth chattered as I scurried through town headed up the north road. And not from the cold, from all these forces freezing the life out of this place.

It was just as close to get to the Chanters' house from the north road or the west road, but I didn't want to go through that west gate again and encounter those lines of soldiers.

Soldiers! Here in Skundton. And not to defend the people, or they would be gathered around the stone circle, but to enforce their will on us. If they thought that would stop Allie

Hunter, they should have brought a lot more soldiers. If I had to sneak around under their noses then I would do that – rat cloak and all.

What had Olen Chanter thought he was doing bringing them here? Had he forgotten where he came from?

But maybe it wasn't entirely his fault. Maybe this was all set in motion when a mayor was elected ten years ago – the night he told me I wasn't Hunter anymore.

Where *was* good old Mayor Alebren?

Hmmm.

I was so rattled that I nearly ran into Goodie Thatcher on the street. I stumbled to a halt just in time to avoid a collision. She looked worn. And old.

"Where are you off to so hastily, Allie Hunter?" she asked, but the bite her words used to carry was gone.

"You need to get out of town, Goodie Thatcher," I replied, trying to do my duty despite the spike of hatred I felt at the sight of her. "These soldiers are dangerous."

Her expression was unreadable.

"A war is coming and they're bringing it right into town," I told her, trying to push her into action. "Everyone knows you gossip. Go gossip around town and tell people to get out of here. To head down the mountain and to the valley kingdoms – to go wherever they have to. But they need to flee before it's too late."

She sniffed. "Tell them yourself."

I grabbed her sleeve. "By the time they think to listen to me it will be too late, but they'll listen to you!"

"I do no favors for Hunters," Goodie Thatcher said, putting her nose in the air. "You're what brought this trouble in the first place. It's my daughter and son-in-law who have to clean up your mess."

"But it's not Olen making those decisions anymore," I insisted, not caring that anyone passing us in the street might hear. "It's this new Sir Eckelmeyer. And he doesn't care about Skundton. He won't listen to you or to Olen or to anyone!"

She shook her head. "You're ten years too late to change this, girl. And I certainly won't be joining you. Go off to the valley yourself if this town is too rich for your blood."

I made a frustrated sound in the back of my throat, but she pushed past me, knocking my blindfold loose and, ambling through the drifting snow, not noticing as it gathered on her shawl and greying hair. My eyes nearly popped out of my head at the sight of the edges of her fraying and tangling as if she, too, were slowly becoming Fae.

What was going on in Skundton?

I blew out a worried sigh, my eyes fixing on the old inn at the center of town. Across from Olen's fancy new house and barracks. Despite the quiver in my belly at the sight of a stream of soldiers carrying supplies to the barracks, I planted my hands on my hips and strode back the way I came toward the inn. Before, it had been the only inn in town. Now, I could see that the old Thatcher home had been made into another inn and so had the Cobblers shop. They'd likely both relocated further down the road. Why hadn't I paid attention to that before? Why hadn't it seemed important who had been moved and who was in the center now?

The old inn had a brand-new sign that said "Alebren Inn" – never needed before in a town with just one inn. I crossed the frozen mud of the street to the Inn, ducking under the sign and through the hand-worn doors into the inn.

The common room was shockingly full for so early in the morning. Serving girls bustled from table to table with tea and hot porridge steaming in the crisp morning air, though a fire roared in the hearth and a cook called from the back to tell the girls to hurry. I didn't recognize a single person in the throngs of those eating breakfast or among the serving girls.

One of them stopped in front of me, a tray of dirty dishes in her hands. "What do you want, girl?"

"Mayor Alebren," I said boldly.

"In the back." She gestured toward a door. "But he's not hiring if that's why you're asking."

I nodded my thanks and then pushed my way past a sweating man who smelled of fresh-cut logs and a table of men with straw sticking to their woolen clothes – likely carters – to the back room.

I flung the door open. I would be taking no nonsense or back-talk from the mayor. This time, he would listen to me.

By the time I closed the door behind me, blocking out the bustle of the common room, I wasn't so certain.

Mayor Alebren was there, alright. Slumped in his chair with a mug of something that smelled sharp and hot all at once.

"Mayor Alebren?" I asked.

He looked up with watery eyes. "No one has called me that in a long time, girl. It's all Knight this and Queen that."

I snorted. "Well, what did you think would happen when you sent for help instead of fighting your own battles?"

His eyes narrowed at me. "You're that Hunter girl. Come back, have you?"

I looked around his cluttered office. There was no window and the only candle guttered and smoked. Blankets were piled over a tufted chair in one corner and parchment was heaped on the desk beside a bottle with the same scent as his mug.

"Don't you ever leave this room?" I asked, aghast.

"Don't need to leave. Inn is fine." He took another drink.

"And what about the town? You're the mayor!. Do you even know what's going on? There's going to be a war. People are going to die. You need to go out there and warn them. Tell them to flee and take their families with them down the mountain to the plains below."

"What's it to you?" There was a slur to his words.

I pressed my lips together, strode forward, grabbed his mug and threw the contents on the floor.

"Hey!" He pawed at the mug and I let him take it back.

"Enough of this!" I said, but I wasn't sure if I was furious or hopeless now that I saw him like this. He wasn't in charge of anything anymore. He hadn't even left the room long enough to hear I was back. And Goodie Thatcher was no longer the queen of society in Skundton.

Why hadn't I noticed that in all these days?

I'd been blinded by my family's troubles and by trying to get back into the Faewald, by the new people and Olen's new station, by the loss of everything I ever knew and I just hadn't realized that the changes ran even deeper.

"You spilled my drink."

I grabbed his fat chin, tipping it up. "You're the mayor of Skundton. This is your responsibility. Rally your people. Take them to safety while you can."

"You do it," he said, swatting my hand away, his head hanging forward and chin on his chest. "If you care so much, you go rescue people who don't want to be rescued. They don't want you. They don't want me. They want knights and queens and they don't care anymore that the Fae are coming to gnaw on our bones."

"You know that?" I asked, breathless. "You know that they are coming to kill everyone. Mayor?"

There was a snort and his head lolled. He had passed out.

I slammed my fist on his desk. Even that didn't wake him.

Skies and stars above! Would no one help save this town? Was I the only one who saw what they refused to see?

Cursing, I left him alone to his uselessness, pushed my way through the common room and back out to the street. There was no one with authority in this town except the knights and they'd made their agenda pretty clear. I couldn't save this town. It was too late for that.

But there were still people I could save.

It was time to focus and to do what I could while I was still free to do it.

New energy filled me as I strode down the road toward the Chanters' house. I just needed to recover the things I'd hidden in the bushes and then I'd be off to save *someone*.

Chapter Seventeen

"Little Nightmare! Can you hear me?"

I slipped behind the nearest tree, my heart hammering in my chest as I pulled out the mirror and Scouvrel's face swam blurrily into view.

"Shhh!" I said, looking one way and another but he didn't listen.

"Your sister's army gathers in the Unicorn Steppes," he whispered, his eyes darting to the side as if he was afraid to be overheard, too. "The Feast of Ravens comes quickly. If you have a plan to end this, you must act quickly."

"I don't know what to do other than to put her in a cage, but to do that, I need to get back to the Faewald," I said, stealing a careful glance around the tree. I heard a scuffle on the path, but I didn't know if it was a person or my imagination.

When I looked back, he was gone.

I cursed.

I did not have enough information.

And I still hadn't opened a path to the Faewald.

My heart hammered in my chest.

The people of two worlds had only me to hope in to prevent a war and I felt woefully inadequate to do it. But I still had to try. Because that's what it meant to be Hunter. It meant that if something threatened your village you *had* to hunt it. And right now my village was being threatened within and without by two separate armies.

Which meant that I needed to hunt them. One way, or another.

Chapter Eighteen

It hadn't taken long to recover my things from the bush or to go get the sword and cage from the tree where I'd hidden them.

"You were gone a long time," Vhalot had growled when I picked her up.

"I had things to attend to."

"I hope you killed someone for me," she had said with a laugh.

"It came close to that."

"How disappointing. Next time, make sure to complete your kill."

It was still early in the morning when I had snuck into the Chanters' house and tapped quietly on my parents' door.

"Yes?" My mother whispered, cracking the door so I could see her.

"You need to take Dad and leave this town. Take the Chanters, too, and every child and innocent who will go with you."

She opened the door the rest of the way. "It's not so easy as that, Allie."

"War is coming," I told her. "Sooner than you realize. I've tried to talk to Mayor Alebren and Goodie Thatcher. I've tried to talk to Olen. I've tried everything and no one is listening to me. Maybe they'll listen to you. We need to get everyone vulnerable – all the children, all the ones with troubled minds, all the elderly – out of this town while we still can. You want me to deal with my sister? I can't do that and also get these people to safety. Help me. Help me by getting as many people as possible clear of this."

She looked at me with compassion. "Allie, you were in the Faewald for ten years. You thought it was a week. If they really are planning to invade our world, it could take them months to pull together their forces, right?" I shrugged and she kept going. "You'll be an aged grandmother before they come back here. I will be long dead. There's no point fleeing an invasion that's likely to never come."

"It's coming," I said, and I could feel my hands shaking with pent up frustration. "And I need your help. I can't do this on my own and I have no one else to turn to. Please, Mother. Please help me."

She bit her lip. "I'll try."

"I know a safe place where you can take them all, but it must stay secret. It must stay safe. Tell no one until you lead them there. Do you understand?" I quickly explained how to get to the covered wagon that would lead them to the Travelers and she nodded along as if she already knew it was there. Maybe she did. The older village women kept secrets.

"I'll try, Allie," she assured me. "I'm proud of your determination, daughter."

I'd pulled her into a hug, shoving down my sizzling energy so I could embrace this moment. "I love you, too."

Fuel, Allie. Use it as fuel. All the frustration. All the desperate need to succeed – let it fuel you.

There was nothing more I could do for any of them. I had to trust my mother with the village children. And I had to do my part for the rest.

Which was why I was standing now on the edge of the stone circle, a cage and axe handle tied to my belt, wearing the clothing I'd worn from the Faewald, my pack and bow slung over my back and a rusty sword held in both my hands.

A bird whistled in the pines on the edge of the mountain plain, his lonely call echoing across the snowy field. I could barely see the pines in the heavy falling snow. Phoenixes had come from this stone circle before. What had ever happened to them?

"What are we doing, Mortal?" Vhalot asked.

"Trying to enter your world," I said grimly. "I'm offering you one last chance to bargain with me for your freedom."

"I won't take it."

"Fine."

I closed my eyes, took off the blindfold, took a long breath, thought of the Court of Cups where some of the mortal children were hidden now, and swung the sword.

I opened my eyes in time to see a split in the air in the center of the circle – like a tear in the fabric, ragged edges and all. I stepped forward, grabbed the edge of the tear and ripped and beyond it the Faewald rose in colors brighter, fuller, richer than anything in the mortal world. I almost sighed with the relief of seeing it again. Which was crazy. This wasn't my home.

The towering cedars of the Court of Cups rose before me.

I leapt through the tear before I could lose my chance, landing in the Faewald, my heart beating a thousand beats for every minute and my breath racing to catch up.

Calm down, Allie, think!

Rippling memories of Scouvrel flashed one after another through my mind and I held my breath for a half-second before I came to my senses. I was here for the children, not to find my husband. But there was a tugging feeling in my chest as if a rope was tied to him somehow and I felt compelled to follow it all the way to where he was.

I shook my head, jammed the rusty sword into my belt – good thing it wasn't sharp! – and pulled the axe handle up, swishing it once through the air to light it. It had better make me invisible in the Faewald like the Travelers had promised, or I was going to be in big trouble.

"We're here!" Vhalot said in awe. "Actually here!"

"And unless you want to be drowned in wine like I was, you'll keep quiet. I don't want anyone knowing I'm here."

I swallowed as I stared at the cedar-ringed Court before me. I'd been here once before and I knew there were children here but thinking of coming to save them and then actually being here and wondering where to start were two different things entirely. Which of those windows above me had sleeping little ones in them? And even if I managed to sneak in there – invisible – could I convince them to come with me back to the world?

Cold sweat broke out across my brow, but I cleared my throat, rolled my shoulders and held my head high. I was Allie Hunter. A little problem like not having any idea what I was doing wasn't going to stop me.

With all the purpose born of weeks of frustration and anger, I strode through the maze of boulders and moss toward

the cedar-enshrouded Court. I wondered – with my spine tingling – if Hulanna might be here despite Scouvrel's warning.

Chapter Nineteen

It took longer than I'd expected to make my way to the main gates, but when I arrived, I paused, shocked by what I saw. Last time I'd been here there were guards at the gates. Last time, this Court had been bustling with people. This time, it was empty. A red handkerchief tumbled down the street, whipped up by the wind. The windows hung open, curtains blowing in the breeze. Nothing was burned or broken. It was just empty.

I walked down the main street, looking this way and that. It wasn't a trick because they couldn't see me. There was simply no one here. I made my way slowly, all the way up to the Great Hall where I'd been imprisoned before, to the very throne room I'd been contained in. There was a thin layer of dust over it, as if people had been gone for more than a week. There weren't even golems working. Last time they had been everywhere, hard at work dusting and polishing, serving and child-kidnapping. Where were they all now?

I moved over to the dais before the throne and wrote in the dust.

"Hulanna. Come find me. Allie."

If she came back here, that should give her pause.

I walked over to the window and looked out furtively over the cedar-shrouded city. Everything seemed so empty.

In the distance, I heard a thump.

Another thump.

Raising my torch high above my head, I slipped through the corridors, following the sound. I hurried down a long, curved corridor on the edge of the city wall. Windows spread bright light through the corridor at regular distances.

Thump.

I opened the nearest door carefully, easing it slowly, slowly open and slipped inside, keeping my torch high. This had better work! It had better make me invisible!

The door came out on a sloped balcony overlooking a gallery below. It was decorated with dripping gilding over the edges of each pillar and balcony, fanciful scenes of Fair Folk and mortals battling with huge armies were painted as murals on the wall. And all across the marble floor, sleeping, crying, eating and even playing – were mortal children. One of them threw a ball against the wall.

Thump. That's what I'd been hearing! I'd found them!

Standing on the balcony, looking down at the children, was my husband.

I gasped.

Oh no.

He whipped his head around and my hand rose to cover my mouth.

Quiet, Allie! Quiet! Don't even breathe!

"Something troubling you, Knave?" the voice of the Balance called from the other side of the gallery. "Or do you dislike minding children so much that you aren't paying them any mind at all? I warn you that if you fail to contain them after I leave, I will take your other ear."

"Help!" Vhalot yelled and I jerked back, scrambling through the door and into the corridor. "Help!"

Desperately, I ran to the window, fumbling for the cage.

I had it on the ledge by the time Scouvrel ran out the door behind me, looking to the right and left. She shouldn't have done that. She shouldn't have given me away like that!

"Knave!" she cried.

He took a step toward me. He was barely a pace away.

I opened the cage door at the same time that I shoved it out the window and shook it until Vhalot fell from it, plunging to the bushes below with a scream.

Scouvrel took the last step to the window and I dodged to the side, the cage clanking against the wall. My heart was in my throat. A took two more silent steps away from him, closing the door to the cage as he leaned out the window looking for what had made the sound.

He was working for the Balance guarding the children. Either he'd lied to me before about not knowing where they were, or he hadn't known then and hadn't bothered to tell me since he found out. Betrayal tasted sour in my mouth. I snuck back into the balcony door, creeping up to the railing.

There were at least twenty children in the gallery. So many.

On the other side of the gallery, the Balance leaned over his balcony, peering toward this one as if trying to see what had happened to Scouvrel.

"Knave?" he called.

I bit my lip. I had to be fast. Carefully, I switched my torch hand to hold the cage too, and drew the sword.

Scouvrel slunk back into the gallery balcony with the grace of a tomcat, his eyes glittering with suppressed secrets. What had he seen? What did he know?

He slipped in right beside me. I froze. Afraid to move.

"Nothing of consequence, Balance," he called back. "Merely a nightmare haunting us by day."

He knew! He knew it was me!

I felt like I couldn't breathe.

No time to panic, Allie. Act!

I clenched my jaw and willed the children small as hard as I could. They vanished, filling my cage.

Quick as a hawk, Scouvrel leaned into where I was and winked, his eyes still unfocused as if he couldn't see me, but his wink suggesting that he knew exactly what was going on.

He laughed as the Balance shouted in alarm. I spun away from him, ignoring the sounds of frightened children in the cage, slashed the air with the sword and leapt through the tear before Scouvrel's reaching hand could snatch me.

Chapter Twenty

I'd done it. I'd brought the children out of the Faewald.

And now they were all crying.

I stood in the stone circle for a full minute before I calmed down enough to raise the cage and look at them.

"I'm Allie Hunter," I said. "And I'm going to bring you somewhere safe. Do you understand?"

One of the older children nodded. They weren't dressed for winter and the howling wind and falling snow – wet and freezing – made them shiver. I patted myself all over. I'd left my pack in the eagle tree. That only left what I was wearing and my cloak wouldn't fit in the cage.

With a burst of inspiration, I pulled off my boots and removed my stockings, shoving them through the bars.

"Use those to keep warm," I said. "Like blankets."

"You look spooky like that," one of the little ones said. He was maybe five. "Like a hero ghost."

"I won't hurt you," I whispered. "I'm going to take you somewhere safe. Somewhere away from the Faeries. Do you want that?"

"Is it really possible?" he asked and his big eyes held so much hope that it nearly broke my heart.

"Yes. And we'll try to find your parents."

Now more than one set of eyes was watery.

"If you say so, hero ghost."

"I'm not a ghost," I said.

"I know you won't hurt us. That's why you're a hero," the boy explained. "But you look creepy with your eyes covered. And that's why you're a ghost."

"I have to cover the cage up so that the wind doesn't make you cold," I explained. "Don't be afraid. I'm right here and you can all come out when it's safe. Okay?"

They just stared at me with big eyes, so I covered the cage with my cloak and began the long slog through the freezing winds to the wagons. I could only hope my mother was gathering up the children of Skundton to take them to the same place. At least these children were easy to transport inside my magic cage. I hadn't even considered that I could do that with the children in town. Maybe I should have. Maybe that would have made things easier.

Kidnapping, Allie. You're thinking about kidnapping. I shook my head at myself. But it was for their own good.

But wasn't that what Olen and Sir Eckelmeyer were saying about what they were doing? Wasn't that what Hulanna was saying? Who was to say what was for someone's "own good"? Maybe you had to let people make their own choices. Even if those choices were terrible.

I strode through the cold, thinking about choices and thinking about Scouvrel. Had he betrayed me? Or had he just saved my life?

And what about Vhalot? Had she survived the fall? I tried not to think about that. It only made my belly roll with guilt.

When I reached the wagon, I checked the ground for signs my mother had been here, but the frozen ground remained undisturbed.

I shook my head, hoping for the best, and hurried inside and through the portal.

The Loremistress was on the other side, mouth open as if she had been speaking. Beyond her, a crowd of Travelers was watching me with wide eyes. She'd been giving a speech, I realized.

Well, I had no time for speeches. I cleared my throat.

"You said you owed me a debt," I told the Loremistress as I whipped my cloak off the cage and set it on the ground, opening the door for the children. "This is how you will repay me. I'm going to rescue all the children trapped in the Faewald and bring them here and you're going to help them find their parents. Your wagons travel all over the world. If anyone can find them, it's you."

The children stumbled wide-eyed out of the cage, returning to full size as they slipped out – one after the next like a little line of goats walking up a hill.

The Loremistress was already nodding and trying to speak, but I kept going.

"Don't ask me how long it will take, because I don't know. Or how many there will be, because I don't know that either. Or how you will do it, because that's for you to figure out. But I'm not leaving a single innocent child in that world, do you understand?"

I sounded angry. I knew that. But I wasn't angry. I was just exhausted and guilty and determined to do better next time. I'd saved these children – but not soon enough. And not enough of them.

One of the little girls ran to me, throwing her arms around my legs. I gaped at her.

"Agreed," the Loremistress said.

"Please take care of them," I said in a smaller, more shaky voice as I looked over to the line of children where Traveler adults were already up and busy, wrapping the children in multi-colored blankets, examining cold red toes, wiping dirty faces and offering hot meat pies. For some reason, my eyes felt misty. I must just be tired.

I reached down and lifted the little girl up, passing her to the Loremistress.

"We will," the Loremistress said and the look on her face was warm and misty, too.

Ridiculous. We were a bunch of fools to get teared up like this. And I was expected for dinner with Sir Eckelmeyer.

I nodded briskly and turned before my first tear fell, scrubbing my eyes with the backs of my hands before I gathered up my cage and cloak and walked through the oak tree and back to the mess I'd left on the other side of this magic door.

I managed to scuff up the footprints in the snow to disguise the path to the wagon and then stumble far enough into the woods to keep anyone from finding the wagon before I collapsed into a heap and fell fast asleep.

When I woke, the sun was orange and low in the sky.

Oh no.

It was long past dark before I reached the Chanters' home and tried to pull the sticks and pine needles from my hair.

The door opened before I even reached it and my mother ran out, glancing quickly over her shoulder and then leaning in to whisper fiercely in my ear. "I need one more night. Just a little more time to organize our flight away from here."

Goodie Chanter was on her heels, calling from the porch where my father and Chanter sat humming together, "Allie! Oh, Allie, you're going to be late!"

"For what?" I asked, still so tired that the world seemed to be moving too quickly while my feet and my brain were trailing through thick mud.

"Your dinner with Sir Eckelmeyer! You were supposed to be there an hour after dark, and it is already that! Goodie Thatcher came with the reminder. Heldra sent her! And she sent a fancy dress you are meant to wear. We have to get you in it. Hurry!"

"Wha – ?"

"Please, Allie," My mother said aloud, adding in a whisper. "We need you to buy us a little more time. Just one more night."

I nodded tiredly, but she practically threw me into her room, stripping off my clothing with appalling speed.

"That's my shirt!" I protested as she pulled it over my head. It was all I could do to rescue the key and mirror from my pocket and furtively slip them into my boots – I thought I saw a wink when I drew it out and hoped it was my imagination – and then to keep my own boots. My mother threw all my clothing except my underthings into a pile by the fire as Goodie Chanter bustled in with a long dark green dress.

"The bow must stay. You can't take that."

"I'll leave it in its place when you're done," I said firmly. They were *not* going to take my bow from me.

"Oh, what a lovely dress! Goodie Chanter cooed, freezing for a moment when her gaze swept over my Fae tattoos. She tried to hide her flinch by smoothing the dress again.

"That's far too fancy!" I said. I'd never seen the like except in the Faewald. It practically shone in the light. "Ow!"

My mother was combing my hair like she meant to tear it out by the roots.

"That hair is attached to my head, in case you were wondering!"

"We were not wondering. Stand still!" my mother said as Goodie Chanter pulled the dress up, jamming my arms into it and then beginning to lace the sides. It was form-fitting through the middle with a dipping neckline and puffs at the top of the sleeves. Puffs! Like I was a present meant to be opened!

I was not a gift to be given to anyone!

Not a gift. More like a Nightmare. That thought made me smile.

They should have dressed me in greyish rags that fluttered in the wind or a long black robe with a scythe and a mask with a long nose, or something that suited me more than glowing dresses with puffs.

"Ow!" I protested again as my mother pulled my hair back and began to braid.

"That blindfold has to go," Goodie Chanter said to twin replies from my mother and me.

"No!"

"It's terribly out of date."

"No!"

She shook her head. "Sir Ecklemeyer is an important man, Allie. You need to do what you can to please him for the sake of our town."

"Please him?" I howled. My voice almost squeaked it was so high by the time I got to the end of the sentence.

"Now, the belt. Why does it have an empty scabbard? We don't have a sword. What will we do, Genda?" Goodie Chanter seemed like she might have the vapors right there.

"Calm down," I said in my most irritated voice. "I have a sword. It's beside my clothing as you'll clearly see if you stop trying to make me your prized goat."

"This is important, Allie," Goodie Chanter scolded. "All our lives depend on it. All the lives in Skundton do. Do you understand?"

She gathered up my rusty sword and jammed it in the scabbard.

"Sure," I said grumpily. "But I thought you didn't believe the Fae were a threat."

My mother exchanged a glance with Goodie Chanter. "The Fae aren't the only ones who could cause us harm. A Knight can hold back ... other things."

If I'd had any energy to spare, I would have asked about the other things. What could be worse than an army of Fae? Other than marrying Sir Eckelmeyer. Which I couldn't do because I was already married.

"And you will go to the dinner?" my mother pushed.

"Yes."

"And you will be good to the Knight?" Goodie Chanter asked.

"Define good." I couldn't keep the exhaustion and crankiness from my voice.

"And you won't take that horrible cage and axe handle with you?" Goodie Chanter scolded.

"They stay or so do I," I said with narrowed eyes.

She sniffed. "Well, you're as pretty as we'll make you in such a short time. Now, run, Allie! Maybe you can pretend you're just fashionably late!"

My mother kissed my cheek, whispering. "Distract them for just one night."

"And say hello to Olen for me!" his mother called as the door slammed behind me.

I stalled to my hiding place like an angry cat and stashed my bow and arrows, wishing I could bring them with the sword and the axe handle. At least I still had them – and the sword. It felt better to wear that than any fancy dress in the kingdom.

With a firm nod, I turned onto the path and began the walk to the center of town. Sir Eckelmeyer should know that he was messing with a hunter. And if I had to hunt knights as well as Fae, then so be it.

Chapter Twenty-One

If Scouvrel was here in my cage – still my prisoner and not my sort-of husband – I would have felt a lot more confident about this evening. Social interactions, trickery, negotiations, bargains – those were things he was good at. I probably could have struck a bargain with him to help me with this – whatever it was. Confrontation? Negotiation? Diplomacy?

If I was honest with myself, I wasn't sure where this evening was about to go, only that I had no choice but to try to keep out of Sir Eckelmeyer's bad books. I was only good at slash and hack and run. That was my skill set. But even if I was Scouvrel with all his tricks, even if I was willing to cut off an ear, that might not get me out of this tricky situation.

I stormed into town like a winter blizzard, glad I'd kept my boots on under the fancy shiny dress. It was too cold to be in a dress, even though it was only the beginning of winter, and I already my fingers were losing feeling and my cheeks and ears were stinging before I'd made it to the town square.

My toes ached in my boots, but the cold was nothing compared to the fire that burned in my chest. I had children to save. I had a sister to stop. I had a purpose in life.

These knights would not take that from me.

Neither would the soldiers who clustered in a group of six around the edge of the town at the north road, a bonfire warming them as they watched for danger.

Neither would the citizens in their houses with windows lit while the streets stayed clear of all traffic except for soldiers carrying supplies and changing guard shifts or huddling around a fire on the street outside the barracks. I hoped my mother would get their children out safely.

Neither would the cluster of guards outside the entrance of Olen's house who looked me up and down and frowned before opening the wide doors.

I scraped my boots off on the mat – after all, it was Heldra who would have to clean up the mud and none of this was her fault – and tromped into the house.

"This way," Heldra said, hurrying up to me from one of the side rooms and gripping my upper arm a little too tight as she hustled me to a lit room I'd never been in. "You're late."

Her anxious gaze swept over me and her other hand gripped her fancy dress too hard. It was rosebud pink and had a voluminous skirt and the same small puffs at the top of the sleeves that mine did. Oddly, it seemed to suit her where it only looked ridiculous on me. I looked as if someone had dressed a buck in a fancy dinner gown.

"I'll take that cage and that ... stick in your hands."

I didn't want to give them up.

"I'll return them when you're done," she said, pleading. "If you bring them in there, Sir Eckelmeyer will just take them."

I handed them over and she put them on a shelf filled with lanterns, frying pans and other tools in her kitchen, hustling me back out to the main room as quickly as she could.

"Be on your best behavior," she whispered. "I know that is hard for you."

And worryingly, that comment wasn't snide. Her tone radiated concern for me. Heldra? Concerned for me? Suddenly, I was actually worried.

"Are your children safe?" I whispered back.

Her mouth thinned to a hard line. "They are with my mother. They *will* be safe. I will make certain of that. Now, do your part for Skundton."

That was what everyone wanted from me, after all. I'd gone from Hunter to Sacrificial Goat in the minds of this town a little too quickly for my own liking.

She angled me through the door, pushing it open before her, her face morphing into a welcoming smile.

"Our last guest has arrived," she announced, sliding easily along the backs of the chairs to sit at the foot of the table beside Olen. Spread out between him and Sir Eckelmeyer who sat at the head of the table, were a series of men in tabards, their hair combed and oiled. I could only assume that semblance of decency meant they were officers of some kind who served under the knights. Or maybe they were just the only soldiers who were housebroken. Who could say?

I'd never thought I'd be missing Ghadrot or even Werex. I never thought I'd be thinking with fondness over the strange circus-like Court of Wings or of Vhalot in my cage. I'd rather be in that company than this company.

The men seated at the table wore hard expressions, their hands gripping knives and forks in a threatening way. Somehow the fact that they were dressed like servants of the good made it all the worse that my senses were screaming to me that they were evil.

At least the Fae didn't pretend to be nice.

"I see you found a sword to put in the belt I sent to you," Sir Eckelemeyer said with a glitter in his eye.

Okay, Allie. This was it. It was word-play time. So, what clever thing could I say?

"Make a bargain with me, Sir Eckelmeyer," I said, because I couldn't think of anything else. Besides, if there was one thing I was beginning to get used to, it was bargains.

Too bad this wasn't the room with the mirror in it. I could use a few hints on bargain-making.

I kept a false smile on my face as I strode down the long line of men to sit in the only empty chair – at the Knight's left hand. On his right, a man equally young with a cruel mouth and flaming red hair ate with manners that suggested he'd never seen a dining table before.

"I only bargain with equals," Sir Eckelmeyer said, downing whatever was in his mug.

My heart was racing, my cheeks stinging from the blood racing to their surface, but I controlled the breath shuddering through me. Time to take a risk.

"Usually, I do the same, but I'll make an exception for you," I shot back disdainfully.

Around me, silence rolled over the table like a cloud passing over the sun. Not a fork scraped on a plate or a mug hit the table.

Sir Eckelmeyer turned his hard gaze on me slowly. "And where did you learn of bargains, village girl? You're no queen."

I threw that back at him, fast as thought. "Where did you learn of queens? You're no gentleman."

He froze and it was as if every set of lungs in the room was waiting for his reply to take another breath.

After a moment he snorted. "I suppose hard rocky land-scapes breed hard rocky women. I should expect no less. Fine, I'll humor you. What would you bargain for?"

Good question. I hadn't thought that far yet, but there was only one thing he could give me.

"The safety of Skundton."

There was a whoosh as everyone let their breath out, but they didn't start eating again.

He raised his eyebrows, swirling his mug thoughtfully. "No need to bargain for that. Our sole aim in coming here is to protect this town."

"Then evacuate the civilians. Before the Fae rush through the circle and kill them all," I challenged. Someone set a plate in front of me, but I hardly glanced at it, despite the appealing scent of roasted chicken. I was not here to enjoy myself.

If I was being honest, I was barely managing to stay awake. I needed sleep and I needed it soon.

He smiled slightly. "I'll consider bargaining with you, but first, please accept my hospitality. Eat. Drink. Pretend you are a lovely lady here to be wooed by the greatest knight of the plains kingdoms."

"I don't pretend."

He raised a finger as if to scold me, waiting.

I picked up the chicken leg with my hand and tore a huge chunk off, chewed, and swallowed all without looking away.

"Happy?" I asked.

His nose wrinkled. "Hardly. I can't see your eyes. Will you take down that blindfold?"

The rest of the town was used to it by now. No one even questioned how I could see through a blindfold. I'd forgotten that I would look strange to this man. Strange and magical.

The hair on the back of my neck rose. "I think I like it where it is."

His hands were so fast that I didn't see them move. He snatched my blindfold from my face and the room flooded with darkness. All up and down the table, all I could see were faint spirit outlines and the specters of the people around the table. The edges of them were unwinding, twisting in a spirit-wind only I could see. Had they been like that before they arrived here? Were the Fae affecting the people on the plains as well as the people of my town?

Olen was the most surprising. Where in the past, he had been beautiful and tall in the spirit world and hunched in the real world, now he stood straight in the real world, but his spirit was hunched over itself. The first tattered edge of him was just beginning to unwind.

Heldra, surprisingly, looked lovely in my spirit sight. That was a change.

I shook my head, frustrated by mixed messages and turned to Sir Eckelmeyer.

It was all I could do not to gasp aloud. That was no young man before me anymore. Old and gnarled, tangled up almost as badly as Scouvrel, the Knight was nearly Fae-like in the horror of his soul. His flesh hung raggedly from his bones and his smile, cruel and wide, showed flickers of fire when his mouth opened to speak.

Was he Fae? Was I only seeing a glamor with my magical sight?

"Give it back," I said calmly, quietly.

"I don't think so," he said, spinning my magic blindfold on his index finger like a trophy. "You wanted to bargain with me? Consider this a bargaining chip. Marry me, Allie Hunter, and I will return this blindfold to you and protect your town. Refuse, and I will keep the blindfold and also keep these people where they are, under martial law, for as long as it pleases her majesty Queen Anabetha. Which, since she listens to my every word, might be forever."

Martial law? A lot had happened in the time it took me to rescue those children.

"I don't believe that. In fact, I think you have very little power beyond what you can trick foolish villagers into believing," I said, boldly. I should never have come here. I was outnumbered and outmatched. But I still spoke the truth. "If you had any real power, what would you need a village girl like me for?"

He flicked a finger and before I could react, the knight beside me grabbed the back of my head and slammed my face into my food. I managed to twist at the last second, keeping my nose out of it so I could at least breathe. He kept me pinned there, hot gravy filling my ear as Sir Eckelmeyer leaned forward to where I could see his tangled specter.

"You've been to the Faewald. You know the enemy. You will be my bloodhound to find and seek the Fae. And together we will destroy them."

"I'd like nothing more than to destroy all the Faewald," I said through gritted teeth – though that was not nearly as true as it had been a few days ago. "But why do you need to *marry* me to do that?"

He laughed. "Don't you know? Queen Anabetha has a strict code of ethics for her knights. We must treat those under our protection with dignity. We must care for them and enact rule of law. This includes hired swords and even spies. Do you know who it doesn't include?"

He paused and I inserted a snide remark while I still could.

"Anyone with the sense to stay far away from you?"

The soldier gave my head an extra shove into the chicken. I winced.

"Wives," he said, leaning down so that I could smell the wine on his breath. "A man may carry out any punishment, any treatment at all that he deems just, on his wife. Which is why I plan to marry you. You will be my hunting dog, under no one's rule but mine. You will do everything I order, knowing that if you fail me you will face unspeakable torture."

"And if I'm already married?" I asked through gritted teeth.

Around me, there was hesitant laughter.

"Well, that would be a shame because then I'd have no reason to bargain with you."

And I'd thought Scouvrel was cruel. I was starting to believe that he was almost kind to me. Not to mention that it was hard to negotiate with mashed potatoes starting to get into one of your blind eyes.

"Do we have an agreement?" Sir Eckelmeyer snarled and I tried not to grimace as his spittle hit my face.

"I'm afraid not," I said, not sorry at all despite his threats. "You see, I really am already married, and my husband is a vengeful man. He'd cut off his own ear before he'd let you have me."

And I felt almost Fae since not a word of that was a lie.

Chapter Twenty-Two

They locked me in the cellar.

After the most intense beating of my life.

In fairness, the only beating of my life.

My second sight made everything seem to happen either too fast or too slow so that I braced for a punch only to relax again just before it hit, or I was hit before I knew to dodge it. It made the whole beating a terrible mingling of darkness, mocking laughter, and sharp agony.

I didn't know how many of the soldiers were in on it.

I didn't know if Olen had joined them in their efforts to kick me apart.

I remembered hearing Heldra crying before someone escorted her out. I remembered being worried about her, too.

I didn't know how long it lasted or how bad it was.

With my blindfold gone, I couldn't see my dress, only feel the tears in it. With it gone, I couldn't see if my knuckles were bloody from the punches I'd thrown when I'd tried to give as good as I got. I'd tried at some point – between bright flares of pain – to pull the rusty sword and swipe myself away from here, but someone had stomped on my fingers until I was sure they were broken and I couldn't pull the sword free.

I was most worried about the blood running hot and steady down my face. And the agony that flared in my ribs anytime I moved, making it feel impossible to breathe. And the way my jaw hung down in a way that I couldn't quite pull back up again.

I was even more worried about the panic that overtook me, robbing me of logic and dignity, leaving me sobbing and shuddering and terrified.

I was trying not to think of the pain. I was trying not to worry about how permanent some of these injuries might be. Thinking like that only brought the panic back and feeling nauseated from panic only made everything worse.

"A few days in the dark might remind you that walking in the light is a privilege," Sir Eckelemeyer had said when they were finally done beating me into what they thought was a fit shape for his wife, and thrown me on the dirt floor of Heldra's cellar. I could smell potatoes and onions here. Heldra was a good Skundton wife.

"I'm blind, in case you've forgotten," I'd shot back, trying desperately to be defiant instead of defeated. If I were being honest, I hadn't really been blind until he'd stolen my blindfold. I'd forgotten how helpless that made me feel. I'd forgotten how weak and hopeless and lost it made me feel.

Oddly, they left the sword in my scabbard, as if they were pretty sure it would be useless to me so there was no point in taking it. I wasn't entirely sure I could even draw it, much less hold it up to fight. Maybe they'd been right.

That was hours ago.

I'd passed out for part of it and woken again to the sound of footsteps and something being set down on the ground beside me. The footsteps left and I reached out tentatively, my fingers searing me with pain when I moved them.

Tea on a tray and some bread. My cage. My axe handle.

Heldra had taken pity on me.

There were big gaps between the floorboards. Which meant I could hear the others discussing everything in the dining room above, as I lay on the cool dirt floor coughing up blood and trying to stop my head from spinning enough to rise. Which also meant that now I knew exactly how much Olen had turned on his own. The Fae-taken little traitor.

"Are you certain you can enforce martial law?" Eckelmeyer had asked him. "Are you certain you can keep them quiet and subservient? We need free rein to operate as a unit without this town interfering."

"Of course," Olen had said. "Mayor Alebren knows what is good for the town. As do the people."

"Fine. I will trust your judgment for now. Gather your Elders together in the morning. I will wed that girl before dawn, and we will use her as our hound to storm the Faewald."

If I was going to escape, then I needed to get up off the dirt floor. I only had until dawn – and who knew how far away that was?

I tried to will my body to sit, but instead, my hands only twitched as a pain flared in my side.

Mmmmph. Not good. Nothing should hurt like this.

A moan tore from my lips and I tried to stifle it.

"What was that?" Olen asked from above me, startled.

"Just the girl. A night in your cellar will shake some of the Fae-lover out of her. You were good to tell me of your suspicions about the Fae influencing her mind, Olen Chanter. Without you, we never would have found such a valuable resource."

Olen could go fry in oil. He deserved every bad thing that was coming for him.

"I only ask that when we invade the lands beyond you watch for my boy," Olen said, his voice heavy. "My Petyr."

I let out a sigh. It was hard to hate a man for loving his son so much that he'd do anything to save him. Even right now when 'anything' seemed to include beating me to a pulp and selling me as a fake bride to a knight who was determined to use me as a dog. His words, not mine.

Come on, Allie. Up!

If you'd asked me last week if I would help invade the Fae-wald, I would have done anything necessary to make it so. I would have gone to Eckelmeyer and offered my services.

But that was last week. That was before I saw that some humans were tangled, too. Before I realized that they were just as willing to unleash hate on other humans as the Fae were. Before I realized that my town and the people in it weren't who I thought they were. Maybe they deserved the Fae and the Fae deserved them. Except for the innocent children. Would my mother get to them in time? She'd asked for one more night. I had given her that, at least.

If I was going to do anything valuable here, I was going to need to stop this war because I couldn't be certain that she'd get them out, and I didn't dare be wrong about that.

And for that, I was going to need an ally.

I only had one ally left.

I forced my hands under me, biting back a scream as every finger seemed to point in a different direction. It took all my strength to push myself up. My breath stuck in my lungs, building up agony behind it like a dam. I found my feet, wavering, fighting down a burst of nausea and dizziness. My left hand could still grip things – I thought maybe I had two fingers still working on that hand as well as the thumb.

I felt for the sword handle with that hand and very awkwardly shifted it out if the scabbard and inch at a time. It fell to the floor with a dull thud.

Shoot.

I was going to have to lean down to get it.

My ribs were loudly proclaiming that there would be no bending.

Tears leaked from my eyes as I half-slumped, half-fell to the earthen ground, my hand scrabbling across the dirt until it hit something solid. I grasped the axe, barely fumbling it into my belt. The cage was next. I couldn't tie it. My fingers weren't working. I hooked the handle over my thumb. I felt for the pommel of the sword, lifting it – barely – in my left hand and fighting my way to my feet again.

Just one swipe, Allie. Just one swipe and hope to the skies above that it works.

I swept the sword through the air with the strength of a toddler.

I thought I could see a rip, but I wasn't sure. I should raise the ax. I should have it to protect me from the Fair Folk. But just thinking of slipping it from my belt made me want to cry with exhaustion. I couldn't. I didn't have the strength.

I stumbled forward, reaching with my crippled right hand. Something brushed the side of it. I gripped it awkwardly between broken fingers and threw my weight against what I hoped was a tear in the air.

I stumbled into a brighter world.

BOOK TWO

Sleep little mousey sleep in your den,
Sleep with the mem'ries of when oh when,
Sing little mousey, sing for your sup,
Sing and we'll offer wine for your cup,
Flee little mousey, flee for your life,
Flee for we're coming with pain and strife.
Try little mousey, try all you can,
Hide from our taboos hide from our ban,
But we'll find you little mousey in any hole you hide,
Your flesh we'll strip and your bones we'll ride.
We'll find any family and we'll find any friend,
Their blood to spill and their hearts to bend.
- Songs of the Fae

Chapter Twenty-Three

I managed to slow my stumble enough to catch my balance. The room in front of me swayed precariously in my vision. Tangled knots of roots formed the walls and a solitary window opened where they met in gnarled clusters. There were more clusters surrounding what might have been a door made of the same. I blinked, fighting a burst of nausea. My vision was growing blurry, but I had to figure out where I was. I had to get somewhere safe before I collapsed.

A huge sewn tapestry of a hunting scene covered one wall – though who was hunting who was impossible to tell. A dragon seemed to be flaming one of the Fae who was firing an arrow at an orc who was gripping the dragon's tail in its teeth. Around them, a unicorn and a purple fox crouched as if waiting for their part in the carnage.

Dark curtains flowed on either side of the open window and a pale curtain – white and almost sheer – fluttered in the wind right in front of me.

The light filtering through the open window was pure white, not the joyful brightness of a yellow sun or even the ominous peach of smoke-filtered air.

I'd only ever seen this light in the Faewald. Which meant the sword had worked.

I was here.

Broken.

Without any of my very useful magical items.

But here.

I sucked in a gasp and at that exact instant, the white curtain fluttered in a sudden burst of wind, thrown up so high that I caught a glimpse of what was beyond it.

My eyes felt like they would fall out of my head.

On the other side of the curtain was a waterfall, running down from an opening in the ceiling, rushing over the curving roots to fill a small stone pool. Bubbles filled the pool and steam rose from it in swirling clouds.

Sitting in the middle of the pool – waist- deep – was Scouvrel, his eyes as huge as an owl's. He held a flapping fish in his hands as if he'd just caught it with his bare hands.

"Nightmare!" he gasped, dropping the fish in the water, and then the curtain fell back, and I lost sight of him.

All my injuries hit me like a hammer.

I slumped to the floor.

The water splashed in the distance and someone was very wetly scrambling for something, feet slapping on stone. The curtain parted, and Scouvrel fell to his knees beside me, a colorful banner that looked almost like a flag wrapped around his waist. I supposed it was too much to expect the Faewald to have something as practical as a towel.

Or as practical as an ugly man. Because Scouvrel was certainly not ugly and the beauty of him was almost painful to look at. I'd forgotten that part.

"What have the mortals done to you, Nightmare?" I couldn't tell if that was concern or rage in his voice.

I moaned as his hands ran gently over my injuries.

"What wicked things have mortal men afflicted on you, my little Nightmare? We will take their fingers and string them on a chain to hang over our door. We will sew their ears on our boot soles and walk on them until there is no whisper of them left. We will grind their bones to powder and mix it in our wine."

He lifted me up and carried me as he whispered his grisly threats, holding me against his wet chest. I was probably getting him disgustingly dirty with blood and snot and dirt. He didn't seem to mind.

Stars danced across my vision. I didn't know where he was taking me. I didn't care.

For the first time in weeks, I felt safe.

Whatever else he was, Scouvrel was my promised friend, my promised ally, and my promised husband. I was almost certain he wouldn't kill me.

"Bargain with me, Nightmare," he crooned. "Bargain and I will heal your wounds."

He laid me down on what felt like a bed of down and pillows. My eyelids lifted enough to see white all around me and then they fell shut again. I was too hot. Everything hurt.

I gasped as my breath caught – painfully – in my chest.

"I cannot help you unless you bargain with me," he whispered, pleading.

Darkness clouded my vision. I fought against it, gasping in breath through my mouth as the pain flared in my broken jaw.

"Give me anything you can spare, Nightmare, and I will heal your wounds."

"You," I gasped.

"Yes?" He sounded like he was holding his breath, waiting for any word from my mouth, but what did I have to give?

"You can have my braid," I whispered.

"It is agreed. I will heal you in return for the ownership of your red braid in all its tangled glory."

He leaned down over me and my eyelids fluttered open for long enough to see his eyes shutter closed as he reverently kissed my braid. Something soft touched my forehead as my eyes shut and the pain in my head disappeared.

I felt so tired.

Something soft skimmed across my jaw and then over my fingers. I struggled to open my eyes again. Was he kissing my fingers? I didn't have the strength to think about it.

Instead, I sank into unconsciousness as my pain blissfully fled a little at a time.

All was dark and warm and safe.

I woke for long enough to feel something heavy on my belly. I opened my eyes, saw a tangle of dark hair and a single pointed ear resting on me. He must have fallen asleep, too.

I sank back into unconsciousness.

When I woke, I was in a bed of white feathers. Literally, white feathers – as long or longer than I was. They blushed in the bright pink light flooding in through the window.

"Haunt me, Nightmare. Wake and haunt me forever," Scouvrel said from where he sat on a stool beside the window. He was leaning forward, half a smile decorating his face, my sword on his knees.

"That's my sword," I said thickly. "And I don't remember bargaining that away."

"There is much you don't remember," he said with a sly smile.

I felt my face growing hot. Had he kissed my wounds away or was that just my memory?

I sat up, trying to inspect myself without being too obvious. My injuries were gone. My fingers flexed easily. My eyes widened despite my careful control. What amazing magic to be able to heal someone with a kiss! Imagine what kind of power that would require. And Scouvrel had done it.

My braid was still intact. I lifted it up with a question in my eyes.

"It's mine," Scouvrel said proudly. "And I find I like it where it is. Do not cut it short. It is not yours to cut."

Good thing I liked my hair long.

"I've been thinking about you," I said, nervous suddenly.

"I should hope so. It would be a grievous thing to be entirely forgotten by one's wife."

I licked my lips. "What I mean is, I've been trying to decide what to do about how you married me against my will. I've been trying to decide what that is supposed to mean for us. And if I should punish you for hiding it from me."

"Hiding it?" He seemed genuinely surprised – which had to be acting. "I thought it was obvious. How can I be blamed for your weak mortal mind missing things? Besides, didn't we already discuss this?"

"You're supposed to ask!" I said, aghast. "What if I murdered you because I was so angry that you'd married me against my will? And we have *not* discussed this in person yet."

"And do you find it exhilarating to argue with your husband in person? I'll admit, there's a certain charm to watching your cheeks flare like the sunrise." His eyes smoldered with those words and I barely suppressed a shiver.

"And what if I'd never found out that we were married?" I continued. "I could have married someone else! It would serve you right if I did!"

"You wouldn't do that, Nightmare. Your greatest joy is in driving me into madness and haunting my every dream. Why would you abandon so perfect a victim – even to find another?"

I tried to adjust my ripped dress not knowing how to even answer such shocking statements. Someone had tied the skirt around me in a way that made it hard to move.

"They tore your dress," Scouvrel said, fire in his eyes, though his expression was neutral. "It's hardly a fashionable piece – rather plain and definitely uncomplimentary to you, not a hint of an animal or bird depicted in it – but I find it offensive that another man felt he could tear the clothing of my wife – particularly in such an indecent way. I did my best to preserve your modesty until you could rise and manage it yourself."

"Thank you?" I did not know how to handle this. He'd preserved my *modesty?* He'd kissed away my wounds? What was going on? Where had my wicked Scouvrel gone?

"You regard me with suspicion. Surely, you must realize that such a debt would not go unpaid. I ransomed you before with my ear. I would happily offer an arm for your revenge."

"I don't think that will be necessary," I said, tightly. I'd better mollify him before I found myself married to a Fae man maimed beyond recognition. "A bath will be more than good enough."

He waved vaguely at the open door and I hurried over to it, fighting my too-tight skirt. The waterfall was still full of bubbles and steam poured from it.

"How is it hot?" I asked.

"Two rivers feed it. One naturally hot. One naturally cold. It alternates depending on which flows most strongly." His eyes danced with teasing. "Rather like you and I, dear Nightmare. One runs hot and one runs cold but which is strongest? Which one dominates? It changes from one moment to the next."

I cleared my throat. "I came here with things. The cage. An axe handle."

He laughed. "Are you afraid I'll cage you like a bird? I've already played that game."

I nodded. "Truth or lie? You like playing games with me."

"Truth. Now, bathe as much as you like. I will take the list of the names of your offenders any time you are ready to offer it."

"I only knew two names," I said, stalling. The water looked good. And since Scouvrel remained in the other room, I stripped my ruined clothes off and sank into the hot water with a satisfied sigh. Dried blood and dirt left clouds of dirty water around me.

Scouvrel materialized a moment later and my hands flew up to cover myself despite the bubbles.

"If I wanted to look, I'd bargain for the privilege," Scouvrel said with a snicker.

Great. Which totally helped my hot cheeks.

His eyes met mine, bright with anticipation. "I want those names."

"Then bargain for *them*," I suggested.

He laughed. "I have missed you, Nightmare. I have missed your defiant looks and taunting games. Though you haunted all my dreams. Though you were with me at every moment these past months. Though I loved my tiny glimpses of you through the Looking Pearl, still I have missed the tension, the fury, the delight of your refusal to bend to me."

"How long has it been?" I asked, feeling light-headed. I was losing time every time I went back and forth between these worlds. Everyone else was living without me.

"Six months. Six months of servitude and the desperate loneliness of a tangled heart." He paused, tilting his head to the side so that the scar where his ear had once been was easy to see. Now, why didn't he glamor that away? "What will you take for those names?"

I grinned. I'd missed this, too, though I hated admitting it. Missed the way his eyes lit and the way his mouth twisted like a drawn bow when he smiled.

"I'll take *your* name," I said.

"You have that already," he said, leaning over the edge of the pool as if he were a lodestone and I the iron.

"Your *real* name."

He drew back, clearly shocked, but at the same time, a smile played across his lips. Perhaps he found me indecently delightful.

"Impossible."

"Well, you did marry me," I said. "You can hardly expect me not to want to know my husband's name."

He scowled. "And you will not allow me the means to hunt my enemies until I offer myself up like a goat for slaughter? That hardly seems like a wifely loyalty."

"If that's how you want to put it ... yes."

"You vicious Nightmare," he said with a look that was both enraged and delighted. "You horrible, gut-wrenching addiction. If I could be rid of you by plunging myself in the darkest depths of the sea, I would not hesitate to drown in the forgetting."

He stormed out of the room dramatically and I took the opportunity to finish scrubbing my face and hair, untangling my braid to wash the dried blood and mud out of it. Would I have survived those injuries if Scouvrel hadn't healed me? I suspected that if I had, I would have been crippled for life. Those fingers had been broken badly. So had my jaw. I shivered at the thought.

I owed him for that. I was going to have very long hair.

When I emerged again from the water, Scouvrel was back, holding up an outfit for me with his face turned away. His consideration for my modesty was humorous when compared to his absolute violence of nature.

The clothing consisted of a shirt as filmy as a white could be with strange lace woven to look like crowns and spiders along the neckline. In his other hand was a dark jacket sewn all over with red snakes. Dark red leggings and thigh-high black boots sewn with black pearls and what looked like fish eyes in patterns up the sides came next. Last of all, was my sword back in the scabbard, the leather of the sword belt was flecked with dried blood. Mine.

"They sully you with torn clothing, but I restore your glory," Scouvrel said proudly. "They try to take your pride, but I elevate you to the ranks of the Sidhe."

"Wait." I felt lightheaded suddenly. "You don't plan to make me Fae, do you?"

I took the clothing from his outstretched hand, studying the back of his head.

"I would not ruin you by condemning you to my hell, Nightmare. Oh no, better that you torture me with your light. I do not wish to sully you in any way. This, I swear on my soul."

"I'm not entirely sure you have a soul," I said cruelly.

"See? We understand each other entirely, Bewitching Nightmare."

"I'm not convinced of that," I said dryly. "Truth or lie, those endearments of yours are nothing more than deception. You are trying to guide my head into a snare I do not see."

His answer came in a whisper. "Truth."

I shuddered.

His voice turned brisk. "Dress quickly, Nightmare. My master comes with the dark."

"The Balance?" I asked.

"Did you forget that you sold me into servitude, my dearest Nightmare? I have not forgotten. I remember every night as I am forced to work his will and not my own. And how it pains me to serve my opposite, chaos serving order and watching as all becomes neat and arranged in the most horrifying codification."

"I should apologize," I said, guiltily.

"I would not accept," Scouvrel said looking over his shoulder at me half-dressed but decent, his expression deeply offended. "I prefer cleverness over compassion. I prefer a wife with a mind as bright as a glow bug to one leaking all over me with her tears."

He leaned in close to me, inhaling as if the scent of me fueled him somehow. Oh. I'd forgotten about how the Fae fed off my emotions.

"I plan to steal the human children from this realm," I reminded him, making my expression fierce and certain.

"Good," he said with a reckless smile, his eyes barely inches from mine. "But don't expect my help. My will is tied to the Balance for a half a year more – thanks to you, you horrible slave trader. Which is why I should not tell you that the rest of the mortal children are kept in this very Court. That would be a terrible betrayal. And also why I shouldn't tell you to go find your sister's hideaway on the Hawkside Cliffs. She keeps her secret things there. And you will want to know the secret she's keeping. But it was not I who told you that."

He leaned in and kissed me so quickly that I barely had time to gasp – a hungry kiss. A dangerous one. It made my blood hot. His wink only made me more shocked.

"I owe you payment for that later," he said breathlessly.

And then he was gone before I could respond. I finished dressing, buckling the scabbard of the sword over the tight trousers and shrugging on the short jacket. How did he always have women's clothing lying around? And how did they always fit me? I should ask more questions. But when he was near me, it was hard to remember to ask.

The moment I was finished, he crept into the room like a shadow, holding his finger to his lips. He leaned in so close that his lips brushed my ear as he whispered. "Hide behind the tapestry until I leave, Nightmare. And do not take so long next time before you come to haunt me again. I will be feeling your breath on my neck and your icy hands around my own in every nightmare I have for many nights to come."

Before I could reply, he shoved me behind the huge tapestry, and I heard his door open with a crash. It was all I could do not to rush out and stab the Balance with the rusty sword hanging at my hip.

Chapter Twenty-Four

I waited long moments until the door slammed shut again and I sucked in a careful breath, gathering up my cage and axe handle. I owed Heldra for getting these to me. Without them, I'd have no chance at all to save the rest of the mortal children.

That they were here in this Court was beyond lucky. But I was starting to wonder about that sword. It seemed to know precisely where you needed to be – and take you there.

I was already regretting not pushing Scouvrel to tell me exactly where the children had been. The man was like that waterfall, running hot one minute and cold the next. What should I conclude from his healing me one minute and admitting that he was planning to snare me the next? Or from him helping me to find the children but refusing to heal me without a bargain in place? He made my head spin.

I shook it violently. I had no time to speculate. I had limited time to find these children and rescue them before my sister invaded the mortal world. I had to hurry. The best way to find a thing was to look.

I crept out from behind the tapestry. There was no one in this bathing room. So far, so good. Sneaking over to the bright window, I looked out and gasped.

The window was cut into a towering chalk cliff wall looming over a tumultuous sea. The last rays of sunset painted the bay a bright pink. Since I was positioned at the very center of a horseshoe-shaped bay, I could see all around the cliff walls. Dozens – maybe even hundreds – of brightly colored cloth bags hung from the cliff walls, suspended by ropes of varying lengths. What in the world could those be?

One of the nearer ones kicked and a brief outline of a human body was suddenly apparent.

No.

I'd heard about these the last time I'd been to the Faewald. These were the Fae who had been punished by being hung in silk bags until they died.

I shuddered.

Whenever I thought I knew how horrible the Faewald could be, it surprised me again.

If I snuck out of this room right now and I was caught before I could use the sword, that could be me. Carefully, I drew it from its sheath. I needed to be ready to escape at a moment's notice.

Here we go. I lifted the torch, swiping it through the air to ignite it. So far, so good.

I strode through the bathing area to the bedroom, ignoring the white feather bed and the sudden images that sprang to mind of a dark head resting on me as I healed, and crossed to the door, inching it open as I braced myself for the squeal of hinges.

No squeal. Well and good.

I slipped into the room beyond and gasped.

The room was enormous. Bigger than Skundton. Whatever tree, or trees, it was built under must have the most spectacular root system imaginable. Roots hung down like hair from the earthen ceiling so high above that my second sight couldn't pierce all the way to the top. Large roots tangled down what I could only think of as cave walls and a spiraling ramp had been carved into the thick earth all around the sides, the roots carefully tied into clumps and clusters that served to hold the ramp in place and direct them to support rather than destroy the structure cut into the white chalk.

Doors opened all along the ramp – doors just like Scouvrel's – and lanterns hung along the ceiling over the curving ramp. Though ceiling was the wrong word because when I looked across the vast space to the other side of the spiral I could see that the walkway spiraled up and up so that each layer of doors stood over the next walkway and layer, making the lanterns appear like a thousand fireflies.

In each of them, a small magical creature like a miniature dragon fluttered inside. So brightly they shone, that I could not look at them for more than a second. And each was its own strange hue – some only white, others blue or purple, aqua or yellow and still others black and yet somehow made of light. I shook my head. Just as the Faewald was full of horrors, it was also full of wonders. Between each door along the ramps were carved shelves and the shelves were so full of bound books that they did not just fill the shelves but had also been wedged on top of other books in any way possible so that one would almost have to fight to pull a single book from a shelf.

Knives hung everywhere: suspended from the ceiling on chains so that they dangled point-first over my head, driven into the walls between the books and along the frames of the doors, decorating the tops of the dragon-lanterns, forming the uprights of the railing that rimmed the spiral ramp and tangled in the roots of the trees

I examined the nearest shelf and my eyes fell on a large black-bound book. I drew it out and opened it and bright blue light flooded my gaze. Surprised, I slammed it shut.

"Studying our sins?" an amused voice asked.

I spun, gasping. I'd been seen.

The walkways were busy. Fae strolled together, lost in conversation or sat on benches along the banister lining the ramp, reading books or sipping from steaming hot cups of tea. Golems shuffled eerily between them carrying books back to the shelves or silver trays of tea.

They seemed to part for my questioner, but none of them looked at him. None of them looked at me.

"How can you see me?" I asked, shocked.

He had been the first Fae I'd ever seen and I would be lying if I said I didn't hate him.

Cavariel smiled that smile I'd found so heart-poundingly gorgeous the first time I'd seen it. It made me feel ill now. He seemed to flex something and his dragonfly wings shot out of his back to flitter in the hanging lights.

"I have a little trick up my sleeve, too," he said with a smirk, pushing up the sleeve of his doublet to show me a silver bracer studded with cabochon rubies. "It makes me invisible. And apparently, it shows me other invisible people. How fitting. After all, you were always the invisible sister, weren't you? Or at least, that's what Hulanna always said."

I felt the blood draining from my cheeks.

"What are you going to do?" I asked him.

"The Court of Knives is a good place to find penitence. I'm sure the Lord of Silk will help you do that if you ask."

It was a threat. And I did not care for it.

"I'd rather not," I returned tightly.

He shrugged. "Then maybe all I want to do is talk."

"I doubt that," I said. "As mired as you are in games of power, you must want more than that."

He looked around carefully, but no one was paying us any attention. Not with Fae everywhere plotting and whispering just like we were. He leaned closer.

"And here I was led to believe that mortals cared very much for their young," he whispered and the feel of his breath on my ear made me gag.

And yet.

"You know where mortal children are in this place?" I whispered back.

His smile twisted my guts, "Bargain with me and I'll show you where they are. One conversation for my guidance. One chance to get to know each other. We're family after all."

"Are we?" I countered. "Has my sister finalized your marriage?"

"Years ago," he drawled. "And what a lovely time we've had, and yet I find I grow tired of her ruthless ambition and single-minded focus."

"Bring me to the children, immediately, without revealing me to anyone else, or harming or killing them when we arrive, or harming or killing me along the way and I will talk with you along the way," I offered.

"It is agreed," he whispered, and his smile had a note of insanity to it and of anticipation that made me sorry that I'd offered at all. "Follow me."

Chapter Twenty-Five

I followed Cavariel through the spiral down, down, down past more Fae than I'd ever seen before. More antlers and bright eyes, more dark sneers and mischievous grimaces. We passed a white tiger in a cage who shot a paw out through the bars and tried to snatch me up. I batted his paw away with the rusty sword.

"Mousey, mousey," Cavariel said dryly. "So many mouseys under the hill."

"Mouseys?" I asked, letting my tone grow equally dry.

"Who but a mouse would hide in a hill? Hide under the Lord of Silk, hoarding up crumbs, when all the rest of the Faewald goes to war?"

"Who?" I asked.

"That's the riddle," he said gleefully. He wasn't what I expected. He stole a cup of wine from a table beside someone's elbow and tossed it back, reaching into his doublet to pull out a little round silver compact and from it to pull a pinch of inky blue dust and snuff it up his nose.

I tried to ignore his strange behavior. How long had it taken my sister to accommodate to these strange ways? Maybe she had liked them from the start.

I tried to ignore the other spectacles as we worked our way to the belly of the cave – the mermaids carried in saltwater filled clam shells almost as wide as the spiral ramp, borne on the backs of golems. Flightless birds ridden by winged Fae which bugled like elk. Unicorns prancing with feet high as if dancing.

I shivered at the sight of those – I knew their secret. But I tried to ignore them all to puzzle out Cavariel's riddle. Did he mean that those gathered here were the ones who *didn't* want to go to war with the Court of Mortals and that the Lord of Silk ruled over them?

"Why does the Lord of Silk rule the Court of Knives?" I whispered when only golems were nearby.

"Swish swish, slash slash, he cut the others' throats. A bag of silk, a long steep fall, they fled this life – one and all!"

Well, that was interesting.

"And everyone who isn't here is going to war?" I prompted.

"Well I am here, and I am most certainly going to war. Outside the lions roar – their battle is to come. Inside the mousey's hide. They do not like the fun."

I nodded. So, this was everyone who wasn't planning to fight my people. There were a lot of Fae here – but given the numbers Scouvrel had revealed before, this was maybe one in ten of their population. I felt cold sweat breaking out over my body. The rest were going to overrun Skundton like a kicked antheap.

And I didn't know anymore if that was a bad thing or a good thing.

Obviously, it's a bad thing, Allie. You don't want Fae and their cruelty spilling over into the mortal world.

But how was that different than Olen and Sir Eckelmeyer? It wasn't.

Even so, it was up to mortals to clean up mortal messes. Being invaded by the Fae as a solution was like hiring a lion to guard your sheep from wolves. All well and good while he hunted the wolves, but the moment they were gone, he'd turn and tear the sheep to pieces.

"Tell me, mortal sister," Cavariel asked, "Has your husband confessed his crimes to you yet? Has he told you he planted the idea of freedom in the ear of the Lord of Silk and that he then slew his predecessor and slaughtered half his court, tying those who objected in bags of silk and hanging them off the cliffs?"

"He did not," I said coolly. Had Scouvrel really been behind that?

"Did he tell you that it was he who first came to me with the Sooth's words and that together over a pinch of Inkdeath, we hatched the plan to break through to the mortal world and lure a mortal back? That your sister would never have come to this place but for him? That I would have remained in my Court of Cups, enjoying wine and feasting and displays of art instead of marrying a bloodthirsty mortal with conquest in her eyes?"

"Don't pin this coming war entirely on my sister," I said smoothly. "You lied to her. You seduced her. You stole her from us."

"And didn't I do a wonderful job of it?" he purred. "When I gave her The Glory I made her twice the terror of any other to ever walk our Courts. I gained a reputation that day. And I plan to build on that reputation."

He spun me against the wall so suddenly that I forgot to gasp. He pressed his body to mine and whispered in my ear. I shuddered, pushing against him, but he was too strong to hold back.

"I could offer you more power than she has, mousey. Break your marriage bond to the Knave. It's not yet completed. Forsake him and cling to me and I shall marry you, too, and make you greater than your sister."

"You don't even like me," I growled. "You picked my sister for her fair face and rejected me for my plain one."

He laughed. "And wasn't I the fool. It turned out, I needed you both. Come, I will offer you a bargain that will make your soul weep with gratitude."

"You lie," I said evenly, slipping from under his arm.

"It would be to your benefit to listen to me, Alastra Hunter." His voice was silk, his eyes like molten honey. "Your sister seeks your death. Your husband the sacrifice of your soul. Only I still want to save you."

"I'd be a fool to trust you," I said, keeping a careful distance from him now that I was free.

He stopped in front of an ornate door.

"You'd be a fool to trust anyone else," he argued. "Think on it, mousey. Think how I could make you rise."

He winked and opened the door.

And as soon as he did, I forgot all about my sister and my husband because rising from a sea of cots, twenty children of various ages looked up at me with sleepy eyes.

I yanked the door shut behind us, my heart suddenly racing. I'd found them – really found them. These must be all the children not with my sister and I could get them free.

"You look like Goodie Hunter," a young voice said, and I gasped as little Petyr stood up from his nest of blankets. I'd found him.

"Your mamma sent me to get you," I said to him and then I spun and fixed Cavariel with a steely gaze. "Bargain with me again, Lord of Cups"

"I don't think so. Our bargain is now complete."

He opened the door, quick as thought, slamming it behind him. I grabbed the handle, but somehow he'd locked or barred it. Behind me, one of the children began to cry.

I spun around. "Shhh, no tears, little ones. All is not lost."

I lifted my cage and thought of them as small and then, while they were still calling out in alarm, I drew the sword and cut through the air.

"It will be okay little ones, I told them as a tear formed in the air, and I grabbed the edge and tore it, opening enough space to slip through.

Chapter Twenty-Six

Nervous energy filled me as I stepped from the tear into the mortal world again. My vision blurred as I went back to the spirit world here, only the torch I held helping with my blurring, dark vision. I held it up a little higher.

All around me, gaping, stood women and men around steaming buckets of water, laundry in their hands. Or so I thought. It was hard to make out the details with only my spirit vision. Everything was blurry and smeared in my vision except what was lit by the torch. We all stared at each other for a moment and then one woman bustled out from behind a covered wagon, a girl on her hip.

"Allie. You've brought us more children," the Loremistress said.

"Yes," I said, having trouble keeping my eyes from growing impossibly wide. She was beautiful, seen with my second sight, like what I imagined a queen would look like. "But what – ?"

"We put the rocks back in the old circle," the Loremistress said, pointing to where I stood. "We thought you might need that, though it means one of us must make music at all times.

There was someone making music. A lone fiddle sang a winsome tune and when I looked, the boy playing it winked at me like it was our little secret. The fiddle was a lightning-blue but the boy's image moved so quickly that it gave me a headache. I tried not to look too carefully. I was blind here without the blindfold. I'd forgotten how tough that was.

"Oh," I said stunned, fumbling for my cage latch and opening it as I set it on the ground.

"Well, don't think you're the only one who knows how the Shining Ones work," the Loremistress said. "We had ancestors, too. And we've seen a lot more magic than you ever have."

She might be surprised. But I didn't say so.

Instead, I coaxed the children out of the cage, helping teary-eyed toddlers, and terrified older children find the warm arms of the Travelers.

"This is all from the Faewald," I said when they'd all been fed and properly dressed and put to bed.

I reached for Petyr. Should I bring the boy to his mother or leave him here? It didn't feel right to bring him back to that horrible town. But it also didn't feel right to keep him from Heldra. With a sigh, I hefted him up into my back.

"I know his mother," I said to the Loremistress. "I'll bring him home."

She nodded and the wrinkles around her eyes crinkled as she smiled at me. "The ones you brought before are ... haunted. But I'm glad you brought them. Children are resilient. They can heal. They will be well again someday."

"And the children of Skundton? Did my mother bring them to you?" I asked, worry filling me.

"Not yet," the Loremistress said, her spirit eyes full of worry. "But we will watch for more refugees."

I nodded, but all I could think of was my mother wandering through the night with my mad father and a gaggle of scared children. And then that worried thought morphed into Scouvrel saying that he had once been one of these children stolen from the mortal world. I couldn't help but wonder what he'd be like if someone had stolen him back and brought him somewhere safe like this.

By the time we said our goodbyes and wrapped Petyr up for the journey home, he was nodding off to sleep. The Loremistress helped me tie him to my back with a long length of cloth, so while he was heavy and exhausting, I could carry him.

It was a long hike home through the cold and snow. I stumbled many times, barely catching myself in time to keep the little boy on my back safe. I was growing weary. I needed real sleep. At least Petyr was protected behind my back, his little head pillowed on my hard shoulder and cupped by the carefully wound fabric the Loremistress had tied him up in.

I grew more and more grateful for the tall fish-eye boots Scouvrel had given me and the fur-lined jacket as the blowing snow whipped around us. What had possessed him to be so generous with me? Was he taking our strange Fae marriage seriously? Even though he'd admitted he was still deceiving me? He was as puzzling as the rest of the Faewald. And he was a puzzle I'd have to solve later. I needed to get Petyr to his mother and get her and the town children safe. And then I needed to trap my sister. I could do this. My plan was working. I just needed to focus and keep working at it.

All would be well. I just couldn't stop pressing on.

I let the heat of that determination keep me warm inside against the cold of the night. I was so caught up in my thoughts that I didn't notice the smell of smoke in the air until I climbed over the rise and saw the Chanter house in the distance.

Oh, sweet stars! No!

My heart was in my throat as I scrambled up the rise between the trees, my lungs aching as I turned my hike into a run, taking care not to knock Petyr's legs against the nearby trees. I stopped under the tree where my magical items were hidden, grabbing my pack and bow and moving the key and mirror to the pack again. At least it was intact.

The house was ablaze – the fire strange and eerie in my spirit vision – there one minute and then gone the next – and it had burned the house to cinders. No human could be alive in what was left of it. Around the house, soldiers stood, staring at the fire, long poles in hand. They must be keeping the fire focused on the house so it didn't spread. Or maybe they were making sure that the job was complete before they left.

Fury filled me with an equal measure of fear. Where were my parents? Had they made it out alive?

Don't panic, Allie. Don't panic.

I was breathing too quickly, and it was making me lightheaded. I didn't want to wonder why I didn't see my parents huddled with the soldiers in the snow. I didn't want to think about why I didn't see the Chanters either.

They weren't here. Or they were dead. And they hadn't made it to the Travelers, either.

Don't panic. Think it through.

Numbly, I turned from the fire. It was going to be a heavy, awkward walk to town with the pack on my front and the boy on my back. And once I was there, I would need to sneak past the guards to the very heart of Sir Eckelmeyer's power, but there was nothing else I could do.

I fought against the anxiety that made my throat dry and my tongue feel fat.

Carefully, I slipped back into the woods, keeping to the narrow rabbit trails between the trees. It was difficult work as I felt my way blindly through the dark, frustration filling me as what should have taken an hour at most took three times that long as I tried to sneak silently through the world despite my blindness, with only the torch to help. I chose a place to enter town that wouldn't be guarded, slipping between a fence and the back of a shed. I remembered this route from when I was a child – a great place to hide in big games of Hide and Seek. A place locals would know about but all these new people would ignore.

And now the hard part.

I waited at the edge of a space between the bakery and the house belonging to the Tanners. The street was brightly lit, and I'd already watched one patrol go by in a blurry haze. I held my breath and waited for the next one to go by before sticking my head out. I knew there were things I wasn't seeing. Just like I knew that I *had* to get to the house across the street.

There was nothing for it. Sometimes you just have to be brave.

I darted through the street to the other side and clung to the wall of the house, my back pressed against it, hoping there would be no cry of warning. After long minutes, I let out a breath and eased my way down the side of the house to the back door. I tried the handle and it was unlocked.

I opened it quickly and stepped inside, shutting it behind me before anyone could object.

Goodie Thatcher stared at me in shock in the process of still taking off her outdoor clothing.

"Goodie Thatcher," I said by way of greeting.

Chapter Twenty-Seven

S he looked furious. "Allie! I – "

I turned slightly to show her the sleeping boy on my back. "I have your grandson."

There was a strangled cry from a nearby room and Heldra ran out from the doorway, wrapping her arms around her son – and me in the process.

"Petyr, oh my Petyr!"

He woke and began to cry, and it was long minutes before we got him untangled and in his mother's arms and hurried away to the bedroom. Long minutes before Goodie Thatcher put the kettle on the hearth and gestured irritably to me to sit. Long minutes before she sat, too, and spoke in her usual aggravating tone.

"Your parents left in the night with the Chanters," she said grimly. "And Heldra's other children. And my Jal." That was her husband. Everyone always forgot about poor Jal Thatcher. "It was before the soldiers went looking for them and before I saw smoke in the direction of the cottage, so they escaped that at least."

"Were they hurt?" I asked.

"No. They had most of the children from the town in tow. Quite a thing heading out in the snow with crying babes and shivering children. You'd better not have sent them to nothing girl. You'd better know what you're doing. You're the reason my Heldra's been thrown from her family home. They blame her for your escape. And Olen didn't stop them. Said he didn't know whether Heldra was to blame. Didn't know! The trouble you cause, Allie Hunter."

She shook her head with frustration, but it was Heldra's voice that stopped her.

"Mother." Just that. Just a name and Goodie Thatcher melted, resting her face into her hands and breaking down in sobs.

I'd been fine until that moment. But watching the woman I'd long thought of as an enemy crack – watching her sob in defeat. Hearing from her lips how soldiers had burned my family out and run Heldra from her home ... it was like a tether that had tied me to this place sprang free.

Heldra sat down beside me and poured the tea. In my spirit vision, I couldn't see her face properly, but she seemed ... settled somehow.

"Thank you, Allie Hunter. For my boy. For everything."

"Of course," I said.

"Not of course," she said and there was iron in those words. That was something I'd never heard from Heldra before. "No one else did it. No one else could. But you brought my boy back from the dead. I'll never forget that."

She took my hand and pressed a cloth into it. "I stole this back. For you."

I gasped. My blindfold!

Grateful, I pulled it on over my eyes and breathed a long sigh of relief when my vision flooded back. Heldra's eyes were red like she'd been crying for a long time and so were Goodie Thatcher's.

"You need to go, too, Heldra," I said.

She nodded, her eyes glancing back to the bedroom.

"You and Petyr," I insisted. "You need to go right now while you can still catch up with my mother. She can take you to safety. She knows the way."

Goodie Thatcher clucked her tongue. "Your mother doesn't know much, Allie. The Fae army will be bigger than I anticipated."

Goodie Thatcher cursed. "I'm sticking here. This is my land. This is my town. I may be old and done, but I'm not yet giving up."

"What about Olen?" I asked. "What does he say?"

Heldra looked away and her mother cursed again.

"It will be a massacre," I insisted. "No one should stay."

"Are you leaving?" Goodie Thatcher challenged me.

"I won't rest until every child is safe and the Fae army is stopped," I said grimly. "Because they won't stop at Skundton. If they break through the barrier and attack, they'll pour all over our lands and out to the sea and no one will be safe. I can't allow that. There needs to be somewhere that the children can be safe."

The other women were nodding.

"I'll leave right away," Heldra said quietly, beginning to gather a cloak and boots.

"I'll help you get the boy ready," her mother said. "Do you have somewhere to be for the rest of the night, Hunter?"

I shook my head.

"Then drink your tea," Goodie Thatcher said, not unkindly. "You look like you're going to fall over. Every bed in this house is full, but you're welcome to sleep by the fire if you like. I've never liked you or yours, but any enemy of my enemies is welcome to my hearth."

Chapter Twenty-Eight

My sleep was troubled and not just because I was sleeping on the earthen floor of Goodie Thatcher's kitchen. Despite desperately needing sleep, my heart was too troubled for it.

I woke with a start in the night not sure if the idea had woken me or a dream had woken me with the idea hot on its heels.

The sword.

Each time I'd used it, it had taken me right where I needed to be – almost too easily. Could that be part of its magic? If so, then I needed to use it now – while I still could. While the invasion still hadn't begun. Scouvrel told me to go and look for my sister's hideaway on the Hawkside Cliffs. Could the sword take me there?

I climbed wearily to my feet, swaying slightly and gathered my pack, my torch, and my other things. I could use a strong cup of tea and something to eat. Instead, I inhaled the scent of Goodie Thatcher's garlic strung along the kitchen rafters, grabbed one of her sticky buns from a basket on the table and drew my sword as quietly as I could.

It made the sound of rusty metal scraping against other rusty metal. I grimaced – after all, I'd probably just woken Goodie Thatcher in the bedroom – took a bite from my stolen sticky bun, and slashed the sword through the air, hoping I was right and that it would take me straight to Hulanna's secret room before I lost my chance.

The air ripped in front of me, letting in a bright glow and I stepped through the rip, pulling down my blindfold, my heart pounding in my chest.

The room I stepped into was exactly what I would have expected from Hulanna. I froze immediately, listening, trying to disturb nothing until I knew for sure that I was alone. Carefully, I drew my foot from the rip and let it close behind me.

If a windstorm had ripped through this room, it could not have looked more chaotic – which was entirely what I would have expected from Hulanna.

A wide bed so covered in pillows and down-filled mattresses in a tangle of colors filled one side of the room. The table beside it held a collection of used teacups and plates. Clothing – gorgeous dresses, necklaces, tiaras, capes, cloaks, and gloves, were strewn over a dressing table and one side of the bed. A wardrobe door stood open with more clothing thrown haphazardly over it. The wardrobe was so stuffed that she wouldn't have been able to hang the clothes within even if she'd wanted to.

A long table ran the length of the room, pushed up under a pair of broad windows. Above it, a dozen hanging lanterns containing sulky glowing creatures. The table was covered with books and papers stacked so high that one mountain seemed to collapse into another. Random objects littered the mess – a looking glass, a device I'd seen in a book once for measuring ship movements, a vial of something red, and another of something green. A stuffed lizard. Two stuffed owls. More bright feathers than I could match to birds, more shells than you'd expect on a beach, and a collection of eyes that looked far too human floating in a glowing jar.

Ugh.

It was night.

Which made this all the more dangerous as anyone could walk in this room.

I waited one more heartbeat, but when no one came, I took a bite of the sticky bun and moved to the table. Ignore the dresses, Allie. And the weird items. What do you see?

What had Scouvrel hoped I'd see?

I sheathed the sword and let my eyes wander over the papers on the desk. A map of Skundton with arrows running from the stone circle to the center of town and down the North Road. Well, that was easy. Just like invading Skundton would be easy for a Fae army.

What else?

There was a book bound in leather and large.

Curious, I opened it, almost dropping the sticky bun when it flared a bright blue. The pages glowed, words dancing into place out of nowhere and pictures pouring in with them.

Eternal Life or Immortality is not so simple as we had hoped. While we can turn any human Fae and add them to our number by means both magical and horrifying, none of us are truly immortal. For, with each passing day we feel ourselves unwind. While some are able to gather up their threads and tangle them up, weaving themselves back together, some are lost to us in months or days.

Even those with the ability to pull their souls back together find that they are just as twisted as the tatters that are left, inclined in this new state to every kind of twisted imagining and selfish evil. Even the best of us are destined to grow worse as the years go by – or perhaps better. Because those so twisted no longer see the world the same way. They are no longer concerned by small villainies, treasuring their tricks and ploys, delighting in the actions that lie where their words can't, enjoying revenges and slaughters as if they were banquets and balls.

Well, that couldn't be truer, I supposed.

I was about to look at the other papers when the words faded and new ones appeared.

A way out had been theorized, but the chance of success is narrow. Only with the right ingredient can we hope to succeed – two halves of one living whole. Light and dark. Devoted and forsaking. Earth and sky. But twins are not found often, and never in such opposites.

I shivered.

They wanted us for more than the prophecy of the Sooth. They wanted us for the words of this book. This book that my sister had.

Beside the book was a list of people. People I knew. People from Skundton. My parents' names had stars beside them and so did Olen and Heldra.

Had my sister made that list?

It couldn't be for anything good.

I glanced back at the book.

The Oolag. That's what the humans call the two linked souls – the solution to our problem. But they only come once in a century – if at all.

The words faded.

Wait. There had to be more.

Frantically, I flipped the pages but there was nothing on any of them. Just empty pages.

I stopped flipping and more words appeared.

This book tells you the story you need to read, not the story you want to read.

So, what story had it been telling Hulanna?

On the pages beside the book, another note caught my eye.

"Dearest of Temporary Loves,

The Knave has been neutralized by enslavement to the Balance, but we lost your sister. Your sacrifice must be delayed. I have failed in our bargain and will accept the consequences.

Cavariel,

Lord of Cups"

Well, that was creepy. Temporary loves? Her *sacrifice*?

Whatever Hulanna had bit off in this Fae world, it was more than she could possibly chew. And why? For what? Because she had hated Skundton so much?

Was it really so terrible to be human that she would sacrifice everything she loved for this life?

Something squeaked outside the door and I froze. One second passed. Another. Nothing. I let out a long breath.

Think, Allie. Think.

Frustrated, I shifted the papers, but between golem tallies and invitations to parties and little books with woodcut couples kissing on the fronts of them, it was hard to find anything valuable. There was a letter from the Lord of Silk that seemed to threaten Hulanna, her Court and her life if she didn't cede to him. There was another from the Sooth reminding her that her prophecy had a time limit and must be fulfilled "before the Blood Moons" whenever that was. Another letter from

Cavariel that made my stomach twist with how it wasn't-quite a love letter.

He was more horrific every time I got to know him better.

I felt ill.

Under another stack, there was a letter she had started and stopped four times.

The first part was scratched out:

"~~Alastra Livoto Hunter must be killed befo~~ "

"~~To pay your debt, go to the human world and bring me back my sister,~~"

"~~Your choice is simple. Execution by silk bag, or the head of Allie Hunter.~~"

And then finally, scrawled into the paper with such a heavy hand that it was torn in places: "If you wish to be free of your debt, you must bring my sister, Allie Hunter, to the Faewald. Nothing short of that will free you."

I paused.

How lovely. My sister wanted me dead very, very badly.

But who had she written that letter to?

Chapter Twenty-Nine

The sticky bun turned to ashes in my mouth. It was one thing to be the hunter and another thing to be hunted. I felt like the creatures on Scouvrel's tapestry, one creature hunting the other, oblivious to what was at his back.

Carefully, I leaned over the desk to look out the window and gasped.

The moon was very bright as it hung over the Faewald. And the lowest edge of it was stained with a brilliant red as if it had rubbed against a cloth dipped in blood.

The Blood Moons.

Whatever I was going to do, I had very little time to do it in.

I tapped my fingers on the desk, trying to think. Had I found what Scouvrel sent me here for? A cryptic book and evidence that my sister was plotting against me and her marriage to Cavariel was less than a happily-ever-after? I already knew that.

My eyes wandered over the book and more words appeared.

For the Earth to rid itself of the air forever, it must only win the half of the Oolag that is of the air – the violent one.

And for the Sky to take the earth as its vassal, it must only win the half of the Oolag that is of the earth – the beautiful one.

But if some strange and daring soul desires to bring them both again as one, to straighten what is tangled and make crooked

paths straight – then only blood will suffice. The blood of both giv-
en willingly to wash us all.

Well, that explained a bit. After all, I'd heard the prophecy:

One born on a single day in two halves.
One half for the land. One for the air.
One for the rending. One for repair.

Except that prophecy was only a faint inkling of what this book was saying. After all, the prophecy hinted that Hulanna and I could be used to destroy and repair. But this one laid out three paths – a path that would rid the mortal world of the Fair Folk. A path that would make the mortal world subservient. And a path that would somehow cleanse the Faewald.

It was obvious which path my sister had chosen – the one that would destroy the mortal world and make it hers.

And I thought it was pretty obvious which one I needed to chase – because it was possible that I could rid the mortal world of the Fae if I could only "win" my sister – whatever that meant.

I looked down at the cage tied to my belt. I could capture her. Would that count as "winning" her?

There was only one way to find out.

I spun around, meaning to find my sister. My scabbard caught on a dress hanging over something and it fell to the ground, revealing a full-sized mirror.

I gasped at the sight of Scouvrel, battered and bloody, lying on a stone floor. Standing over him, Cavariel held a whip.

"Nightmare," Scouvrel mouthed though no sound came from his lips.

Cavariel's smile was wicked. "Now, tell me, Knave, where your mortal wife has gone with all of our children. Tell me, or I will ask the Balance and he will make you whip yourself again."

I gasped, my eyes going wide with horror as I realized Scouvrel held a bloody whip in his hands. It had seven tails, each with a barbed end. He'd been forced to whip himself.

"You can't," I gasped. "You mustn't."

I fell to my knees, trying to reach for Scouvrel, but my fingers met only smooth glass. This was my fault. I had sold him to the Balance.

"Before you say that he won't force you," Cavariel crooned, "remember that your mortal wife took something valuable from us. As the Balance, it is his role to restore order. He must take from you. How much pain do you think you must sustain before you atone for so many stolen children?"

Behind Scouvrel, the Balance walked into my line of sight through the mirror. He looked cool and calm, the feathers of his white wing were unruffled.

"He could give us the mortal," the Balance said. "That would pay the debt."

"Scouvrel, I'm so sorry!" I said. "This is all my fault."

"Nightmare," he gasped, his eyes glassy, his breath ragged. He tried to reach for me, feebly, his fingers closing on nothing.

"It is a nightmare, isn't it?" Cavariel crooned, not seeing or hearing me.

"They'll drown you in a river of blood," Scouvrel whispered and his glassy eyes met mine. Was he trying to warn me?

"Reliving your childhood, Knave?" Cavariel asked with a laugh. "They did that to us a long time ago."

I shivered.

The door to their room burst open and a golem stepped into the room with a small note in his hand. The Balance sighed and took the note, reading it quickly.

"We'll have to return to your fun later, Lord of Cups. This note is from your wife. The Feast of Ravens has begun."

Chapter Thirty

I bit back a curse as they grabbed Scouvrel and began to drag him across the floor. He reached toward me and for a second I thought he was hoping for help and then the vision of the mirror winked out of sight.

I gasped.

He was gone.

And the mortal world was being invaded.

I had succeeded in saving my father from my sister ... sort of.

I had succeeded in saving the mortal children ... as best as I could.

But I was far behind Hulanna when it came to this great game that I knew nothing about – a game that wagered both our lives with the stakes as high as they could be.

My mouth felt dry.

I had failed to set a proper trap for her, letting compassion rule me rather than cunning. And I had failed to rally more allies. I'd bargained the only one I had away.

My palms felt sweaty.

Which left just one thing.

War.

A war between sisters. A war between two halves of the same whole. A war I wasn't sure I could possibly win.

I flexed my hands and checked my gear. I had the blindfold and the axe handle – which didn't do much good outside the Faewald, the sword and the key, the tiny mirror, and the cage.

Carefully, I took the bow out of my quiver and strung it. When next I cut into the mortal world, there would be a war. I needed to be ready.

I checked my gear, being sure that my cage was ready.

I was going to try to put Hulanna into the cage. All I needed was a single glimpse of her. This was my last chance to do the job that I came here for in the first place – stopping my twin sister. I opened my pack, pulled out the rat skin and threw it over my shoulders, tying the leathery feet across my chest.

It stank.

But it reminded me who I was. I was Allie Hunter. Make me small and I would kill rats. Make me large again and I'd take down the whole Faewald. I did not give up. I did not back down. I was not ready to give up this fight.

On a last impulse, I grabbed the glowing book from the table and jammed it into my overflowing pack. I'd need to clean it out soon. I was starting to resemble a turtle with this thing on my back.

Stop stalling, Allie. This won't get any easier the longer you wait.

I drew the sword, about to slice the air in two when the door burst open and Werex ran in, his face grim.

"Lady of Cups, I – "

We both froze, sharing a moment of shock. I was the first to react. I closed my eyes and imagined him small.

You are nothing, you are nothing, you are nothing.

A tiny pain in my leg made me gasp and I looked down to see a sword the size of a sewing pin jammed into my thigh to the hilt.

I put my bow on the table, yanked the cage away from my body, then pulled out the little sword and tossed it to the floor. I'd forgotten how much damage a little Fae could do.

"Werex," I said through gritted teeth, holding the cage up to where I could see him. "If you have more weapons in there, I suggest you keep them to yourself or I'll get irritated and see how *you* like being drowned in a vat of wine."

His green face looked pale.

"What is this madness, mortal? And what have you done with the Lady of Cups?"

"You're my prisoner now, Lord of Twilight," I said frustrated by the change of events. What was I going to do with Werex? I couldn't let him go or he would just jump out and kill me. I could dump him out the window like I'd done with Vhalrot, but then he might give me away to my sister. Dragging him around with me in this cage was going to be a pain.

With quick fingers, I grabbed one of Hulanna's scarves and tied the cage to my pack. At least that way I wouldn't have Werex jabbing things into my legs. Then I pulled the blindfold over my eyes, trying not to flinch as the Faewald grew terribly spooky and Hulanna's fine room became nothing more than rags and broken teacups, dirty papers and howling emptiness through the windows. Even Werex in this tiny form twisted and writhed.

"Let me out, Mortal!" he called.

"Quiet, or I'll fill your cage with so much iron that you'll burn if you so much as blink."

I grabbed the bow and sword again, and before I could talk myself out of it, I cut a hole in the air and stepped through as Werex hissed at me.

I had expected to come out in the mortal world and I almost choked when I stepped through and the world was still tangled.

Terrified, I yanked my blindfold down with one hand. I had no idea that the sword could take me from one place to another in the same world.

Where was I? The place was empty and had a fine layer of dust over everything.

From inside the cage, Werex was laughing.

"Neither of us has wings, Mortal. What a terrible choice of place to bring us to."

We were on a platform over a massive chasm. Mist drifted up from below and clouds ringed us in the darkness above, blotting out the Blood Moon. No stairs or ladders led to the platform. No structure seemed to hold it in place. There was only a platform which at most could hold four people – at most – comfortably. There was no rail around the edges to protect you from the terrifying drop. In the very center of the platform was a jumble of items. I tattered blanket too small for an adult. A worn rabbit made of tied rags. I'd had one like that as a child. I picked it up and out from under it rolled a carved toad no larger than my thumb. It was so very lifelike that I reached out and touched it.

I snatched my hand back when the carving came to life, its tongue flicking out at my finger. The moment my hand was gone, it fell to the ground, frozen again. I leaned down and snatched it up again.

"A speaking frog," Werex said. "That's valuable. I'll bargain for that."

"What is it?" I asked, examining the strange thing. "And where are we?"

"This is clearly the Court of Wings," Werex said in a bored tone. "How else did you imagine people got to this platform? It's in the Neverending Chasm by the look of things. And we are trapped. Unless that sword can open the air again. Clever little trinket that it is."

I looked at the frog. It didn't move this time.

"Speak, Talking Frog," I said, feeling foolish.

"Don't forget," it whispered in a young boy's voice that seemed oddly familiar. "Don't forget who you are in this terrible place. You're Finmark Thorne. Your father pulls stumps from fields for farmers. Your mother makes raspberry jam. They love you. You have three older brothers, Maveren, Tristarch, and Grimmen and they love you, too. Don't let them make you forget. Don't let them take that from you, too."

It stopped, suddenly and then it was still.

I shivered.

"Did it say a name?" Werex asked.

"Didn't you hear it?" I jammed the frog into my pocket.

"It only says one name. And only the person holding it can hear the name. I'll bargain for it. There's a name I'd dearly love to have. Perhaps the frog has it."

There was a growl in his voice by the end of that sentence.

"You want the name it gave me?"

He smirked. "That would be interesting, mortal. I'd bargain for that, too, but I'm just as interested in the name it would give me."

"And whose name would that be?" I asked, readying my sword again. I'd better not drop it, or I would die on this platform.

"The frog gives the true name of the person most aligned with your interests. It's very handy to know your ally's true name. Keeps them honest. Even more handy to know if they are truly the most aligned with your interest, don't you think?"

So, who was Finmark Thorne? I'd never heard that name before. And yet, my breath hitched just a little as I tried not to guess who I was sure it must be.

Was it possible that sad lonely boy had once been Scouvrel?

"Let's try this again, shall we?" I said, slipping my blindfold back up and slashing the sword through the air again.

Chapter Thirty-One

I slipped through the rip in the air, barely managing to scrape my pack and everything in it through with me.

I was hit with a wall of sound.

Shouts, screams, and battle cries mixed with the sound of feet and hooves and clashing metal.

It had already begun.

My heart was racing to keep up with my ears.

I sheathed my sword, crouching into a defensive position on instinct and turning slowly to assess how much danger I was in. Werex was shouting something but I couldn't make it out over the noise. I ignored him. I didn't put him in that cage for his opinion.

I was in a small tangle of thick saplings, so dense that it was hard to see through them. They completely surrounded me. Right now, that was a good thing. I moved and the saplings squeezed my limbs, making it hard to even maneuver enough to look out of the trees.

I shoved my head through the tangle to look out. I'd expected to see fighting.

What I hadn't realized was that just moving an enraged army led to a lot of noise.

I was on the edge of the mountain plains where the forest began. I had a mostly obstructed view of the stone circle. From it, Fae poured like wine from a pitcher – Fae on antlered glowing stags, Fae on shining unicorns, Fae with bright armor or dark tattoos, Fae with green orc skin and wickedly sharp weapons, Fae dressed for a ball with curling wings behind them. Ready for battle, eager for pain, they rode – every kind of Fae I could imagine, dressed in every way possible, poured from the circle and out over the plain. They settled into streams of armed Faerie following the paths Hulanna had marked on the map in her room.

I strained my eyes searching for my sister.

There she was.

She stood on the saddle of a unicorn, seemingly oblivious to the danger of balancing on a movable animal who kept a sharp horn on its head.

I tried to think of her as small, but all I could see was how powerful she looked.

She wore a gilded breastplate and a gilded winged helmet, her dark red hair flowing in the air behind her and her slashed black skirts fluttering like a flag of death in the wind. She'd worn boots and had a small rune-encrusted buckler on her arm with a pair of stout bracers – these seemed to be her only nod to practicality.

She was beautiful. She was glorious. She was everything I wanted to be.

I tried to think of her faults, her deficiencies. It was like grasping at air.

My sight was obstructed by a horned Fae riding a stag and a horde of the Court of Twilight running at his back.

My heart plummeted.

I'd failed!

I'd planned this. I'd been there at the right moment. I'd caught sight of her just like I'd hoped – and it hadn't been enough. I hadn't been able to do it. I hadn't bet on my own failure.

I stood on tiptoes, trying to see Hulanna again, swallowing down a burst of panic.

Don't panic, Allie. You can still do this. You just need to catch sight of her again.

Beside me, Werex was cursing so long and hard that he'd run out of any curses I'd ever heard and the layer he'd found below those was scorching my ears and making my cheeks burn hot.

There was a roar as someone caught sight of me from nearby and I leapt from the tangle of trees, kicking up clods of moss as I scrambled across land as familiar as the back of my hand, ripping up my blindfold so I could see and leaping from one rock to a fallen tree to a place where the land dipped too much for a stag to easily leap.

I'd lost sight of Hulanna. I'd lost sight of all the Fae. Cursing, I pulled my blindfold down again.

I was running in the wrong direction.

But I had no other choice. I pulled the axe handle from my belt, swishing it through the air and holding it high so I could see. I'd lost time doing that.

The orcs behind me let up a hoot of delight and I ran faster, skidding around the turns and stumbling over tangles of raspberry bushes and mossy fallen logs, trying to stay in the light of the torch in my spirit sight.

Faster, Allie! Faster!

I couldn't stay ahead of them for long. I needed a place to hide. And fast.

Wasn't there a little knoll along here where a bear had made a den a few years ago? That would be a decade ago and more now.

I hurried toward it, zig-zagging, trying to lose them.

Please don't have a bear in you, knoll!

I scrambled through a stand of birch and leapt over the edge of the knoll, turning to push into the small cave. I yanked my blindfold up, but my normal vision showed nothing, and the den felt cold, smelling of nothing but fresh mountain air. I pulled it back down again.

The den was unoccupied.

I tried to get my breath under control. They were right behind me and I only just fit in this little cave made by a tangle of roots above and heavy stones along the sides and back of the den.

There was a shower of moss and earth at the entrance that kicked back over me. I held my torch high and watched as a dozen orcs leapt over the mossy knoll, followed by the glowing stag.

One breath.

No one had turned.

Two breaths.

Whew.

"We're hiding in a cave," Werex said.

I ripped off my rat cloak and jammed it over the cage. He'd better be quiet! He'd better be!

I watched the entrance, fear washing over me, but no one turned around. When my heart finally calmed, I pulled the rat cloak off the cage.

"Quiet or I will make you quiet."

"We're missing all the fun," he protested, but at least he did it quietly.

"Shall I assume you are unhappy with this turn of events?" I whispered to Werex between my teeth. "I thought you wanted a Feast of Ravens."

"I wanted to lead it, not be carried in a cage! The Lady of Cups gave the order too soon. She tricked me."

"Isn't that what Fae do?"

"We also drown people we don't like in wine," he reminded me. "We do a lot of things. I will show her many of them if I am ever freed of this cage."

I snorted. "But you won't be free of this cage unless you do what I say."

"Not a chance," he said.

This cave was as good a place as any to hide my things. I couldn't carry them all with me in the middle of a battle. I slid the pack off my back. What would I need with me?

The bow and arrows.

The sword.

It was cold out there and the rat cloak would help.

I pushed the rest into the back of the cave. I'd have to come back for it.

I held the ax up. If I brought it, one hand would be occupied. I couldn't use my bow. With a sigh, I shoved it into the cave with my pack. The world went dark. I missed it already.

What about the cage. What should I do with that?

"Stare all you like," Werex growled. "I will not change my mind."

"I'm merely deciding whether to leave you here or bring you with me," I said, pursing my lips.

Without the cage, I couldn't catch Hulanna. With the cage, I was stuck with a noisy Werex. It seemed to be an impossible choice.

There was no point in chasing her if I didn't bring the cage. It was my only chance.

With a sigh, I tied it to my belt and left the cave.

Chapter Thirty-Two

The hot chaos of battle was entirely unfamiliar to me.

I was used to waiting patiently, to picking my shot, to controlling my breathing.

I was not used to stags charging through the woods with three Fae on their backs shooting darts wildly into the trees. I'd barely dodged a dart and I nocked an arrow before they were gone, leaping through the trees.

I kept my blindfold down. It made the landscape blurry and nausea-inducing, but the Fae were clear and bright. Better to see the enemy than see every tree and stump.

I'd made it maybe three steps before a group of three orcs carrying axes rushed past. Werex shouted for them and they spun.

Oh, for the love of all that's good!

I shot the first arrow without thinking, picking my spot by instinct – the unarmored throat – and had a second arrow out and nocked by the time the remaining two charged.

A second throat shot. I didn't wait to see whether he dropped.

My hands were shaking.

The third orc was on me. I grabbed the cage, raising it to take the blow.

Werex screamed from within and I turned the blow well enough to leap to the side. I dropped the cage and it tugged on my belt as I grabbed another arrow, nocking it. No time to aim.

My shot went wide.

And turned – impossibly – twisting in the air to hit the target right in the eye.

I gasped as he stumbled backward, quickly grabbing another arrow and firing again. This time, I hit his neck, severing the artery in it. He fell to the ground.

I leaned over, gasping, retching into the grass. Killing sentient creatures was not something I was used to. Not even orcs.

I couldn't calm down. My breath was coming too fast, my head swimming too wildly.

"Impossible," Werex hissed.

The Travelers had said it would pierce the heart of the evil. I'd thought it was metaphorical. It was, in a way, since it had not pierced the heart, but it had turned in the air to find that which was evil.

Magic.

Magic was impossible and frustrating ... and my only hope right now.

Calmly, I lifted my blindfold and collected the arrows, quickly pulling it back down when I was done and watching furtively around me for more surprises. I tried to ignore Werex's loud cursing.

"Who gave you this magic, mortal? It is not for the hands of those of your kind. I shall rend them to pieces and stamp out every last one of their kin."

"Is that a threat, orc?"

"I will do more than threaten. I will gut you."

I hit the cage against a tree, sending him sprawling.

"I said to be quiet," I hissed. "And I meant it. Be quiet, or I will find out if this arrow can slide through those bars and pierce *your* evil heart."

I leaned with my back solidly against the tree, catching my breath in huge gulps. Everything seemed to be too fast. There were knots of Fae everywhere, moving through *my* woods like they owned the place.

My hands were shaking. I couldn't calm them.

I didn't like battle and I didn't like killing.

I wiped my brow with the back of my hand, checked that my arrow was nocked on the string and stalked out from my cover, keeping low, watching carefully.

Why hadn't I just put them all in the cage? Instinct had reared up and demanded that I shoot, but I could just as easily imprison them.

I crept around a rock that stood behind a massive fir tree.

A clash of steel on steel made me freeze, but I shook my head, lifted my blindfold and looked out around the knoll. A knot of about ten humans fought together, Corne among them. They held their shields high, polearms slashing out from the knot, but even with so much thought given to their defense, they were losing.

I pulled the blindfold off and looked again.

Four orc Fae danced around them whooping and laughing as their curved axes slammed into the edges of the shields, denting, splintering and even splitting them. Growling, I focused on the nearest one, narrowed my eyes and imagined him small and in my cage.

He disappeared. Now, why hadn't I been able to do that to Hulanna?

I adjusted my blindfold so it covered just one eye. It made me dizzy, but that was better than blind.

The other two Fae looked at each other with puzzled expressions and at that moment Corne yelled, "Retreat to the barricades!"

Barricades?

The knot began to move at the same time that I heard a scuffle in the cage at my waist. No time for that.

One of the orcs raised a horn to his lips and blew and in the distance, I heard a war cry. A loud crash sounded from my left and another from my right.

Great. They'd be converging here. Right where I was.

The orc raised his horn to his lips again and I thought of him as small, willed him into my cage.

Poof. He was gone.

One of the human soldiers thrust with his polearm at the last orc. His fellows leaned in with grunts of their own and he was down on the ground, bleeding.

I scurried under the fir tree, keeping low. I needed to get to the town. That's where my sister would go. That's where everything would happen. I was just wasting time out here.

I lifted my cage and gasped.

"What have you done?"

Werex stood beside the corpses of the other two Fae.

"Can none of you be in a cage together without killing each other?" I whispered.

"They were in the battle rage. They could not stop," Werex said.

"And you? Aren't you their Lord of Twilight or something?"

"Exactly. It's not my job to act as nursemaid."

The Fae were insane.

And it was going to be no kinder to put one of them in that cage than it would be to shoot him. I shook my head, frustrated.

"Make a bargain with me," I whispered to Werex.

"You'd only ask for that if you were weak."

Something crashed close to us and I flinched as a dozen stags thundered past, leaping over dead trees as if they were nothing and sliding between slender birches like they were born for this. The Fae on their backs were masked like they were going to a ball, their wings fluttering behind them in dragonfly iridescence.

I had to keep moving. I pulled the blindfold down again.

"I'll let you out of the cage if you promise not to kill, injure, wound or capture me," I said grimly. I needed quiet and I needed him gone. Better to release him into the world than to deal with him here.

"You'll kill me once you free me."

"I'll promise not to for at least an hour after I set you free."

He barked a laugh. "Not a chance. If it benefits you, it does not benefit me. I have a feeling that you are a key to solving our little Faewald problem, mortal, in a way that a single Feast of Ravens will not solve it. I'm of a mind to carry on with you and watch."

"In a cage?" I asked.

He shrugged. "What does it matter?"

I sighed.

"I also think you might bring me to wherever the Knave is hiding," Werex said with an evil grin. "And I have wanted him dead for a very long time."

"Why?" I asked, leaving the tree and sneaking to the next clump of cover.

"I mislike the prophecy that was spoken over him during his Glory – that he would 'by great sacrifice and in the giving of what is most precious to him, untangle the Fae.' I like being tangled. I like the Faewald exactly as it is."

"Great," I said. "You sound like a fantastic leader."

He laughed.

I could almost see the town from here as I slipped through the trees. I pulled my blindfold up for a moment to study it.

They really had set up barricades between the houses and on the only road I could glimpse from here. The barricades were manned by soldiers, but there were just as many villagers standing on the shaky piles of timber and furniture and over-turned carts. I recognized boys I'd played with before – men now – and boys I'd watched as children who were about my age now. They looked terrified.

They had every right to be terrified.

At least I wasn't seeing children.

I pulled the blindfold back down.

The Fae hung back from the barricades, arranging them-selves in a circle around the town, their faces almost shining with excitement. They loved this. They lived for this.

"There's nothing quite like a Feast of Ravens," Werex mur-mured happily from the cage.

I spat as my response.

And then Sir Eckelmeyer climbed up on top of a hastily-built scaffold just inside the barricade that stretched over the North Road and my heart skipped a beat.

Chapter Thirty-Three

Sir Eckelmeyer stood on the platform in the center of the town, a bannerman behind him with the flowing white and gold banner of Queen Anabetha in his hands, her golden hawk emblazoned on it.

"Know this, foul creatures," he called out to the opposing army. "Your evil has no hold here. Our Queen has already sent a full battalion to aid us here. You cannot win! Surrender by nightfall or the family of Hulanna Hunter will pay the price."

Was he kidding?

I felt a stab of terror. He didn't have my parents, did he? Had he found them fleeing through the woods with the village children? Had he captured them? Sweat broke out on my brow, but no. He couldn't have. This had to be a bluff.

Werex began to laugh in the cage.

He must know – as I knew – that Hulanna didn't care about my parents. And that I had no way to stop this battle. He was threatening the wrong people with the wrong things. I made a frustrated sound in the back of my throat, but there was nothing I could do. Yet.

I needed to find my sister.

Oh, and I had to be sure I did it by nightfall or every human would want me as dead as the Fae did.

I looked up through the white skies and drifting snow, trying to determine what time it was, but the sky was too thick with clouds to see the sun. It was day. That was all I knew. And I was already running out of time.

I had to find my sister.

I pushed through a tangle of raspberry bushes, scanning the gathering crowd and feeling dizzy with my blindfold half on and half off.

Maybe if I pulled my hood up, I could pretend to be a Fae. Maybe they wouldn't notice me. Maybe ...

A horn sounded. Not like the horn the orc had blown. This one tinkled like small bells, a glorious song that made me feel like I would follow it anywhere.

A shudder ran down the ring of gathered Fae and then, all at once, they plunged forward.

The humans stood firm, unaware of what was happening. Then suddenly their eyes opened. The Fae must have decided it was more fun if their prey could see them coming.

Swords hit axes in a loud clash. Grunts and moans filled the air and I ran forward, staying behind the armies, searching their ranks. My sister was in this tangle somewhere, I knew it.

Another clash filled the air as axes hit shields and tiny Fae crossbows shot out darts from the backs of hinds and unicorns. Hot breath gusted in the cold winter air. Hot blood ran red into the white drifting snow.

No sign of my sister. No sign of Cavariel. No sign of Ghadrot. Or any of the Fae I knew.

Someone shouted near me and I spun to see a Fae on a stag, her eyes lighting with excitement at the sight of me. She began to aim her small crossbow, but I drew my arrow and nocked it in a single practiced motion, loosing it first and rolling to the side to avoid her dart.

Everything hurt. My hands, my ribs. That roll had taken me over a rocky patch of ground. But I was up on my feet again before I could stop to think, leather boots slipping in the wet snow-filled grass.

I scrambled across the slippery surface, running behind the nearest tree and then through the tangled woods and scattered combatants as I slipped away from that fight.

I tried to ignore the screams – far too human, far too real – as I tore past astonished groups of Fae. Their eyes widened when they saw me – rat cloak and all – and they paused temporarily in their laughter and merriment. These edges of the battle didn't look like a battle at all – more like the edges of a sporting event like our Summer Picnic in Skundton where families would bring wide blankets to sit on and sip cool water and eat sweet berries and sliced roasted meat with cheese.

This was a game for them. I was surprised none of them were flying over the town for a better view.

"Why don't they fly?" I asked Werex as we passed a group of winged females, their monarch butterfly wings delicate and lovely as they flicked gathering snow from their wings. "They could seize the town in a heartbeat if they did."

"Can't fly in the mortal world. Too much earthiness. Not enough airiness," Werex scoffed.

"That makes no sense," I said.

"War does not make sense, bloodthirsty mortal. Nor does peace. Love does not make sense and nor does hate. Magic does not make sense. But a life without any of them is a miserable echo of a thing."

"Sure," I agreed, flinching as I watched a boy my age topple from a barricade between two houses. The Fae around him roared, pushing through the feeble excuse for a wall and rushing into the town. "Boring. Just what I was afraid of."

"You've lived too short a life to lecture me," Werex replied. He had none of Scouvrel's sense of humor and all of his violence. "This little 'war' is nothing more than a party game to us. Look at the Fae around you. Are they grim and afraid? No. They laugh and jest and most of them ignore you – one single boring mortal. This is not a challenge for us. It is not a concern. It's just a party. We came to play with the mortals like a cat plays with mice. The cat is not the one who needs to fear."

"Fascinating," I replied dryly.

Through the trees toward the East Road, I thought I saw a huge white stag and was that a glimmer of red hair?

My sister!

I hurried along, sliding through drifts of fresh snow, skirting a group of golems who were painstakingly setting up a striped pavilion. Maybe the Fae really did think this was a party. I could have sworn that was a crate of wine bottles one of them was carrying.

There were peals of laughter from the other side of the pavilion and then a horrific scream. I rounded the tent cautiously, keeping from view.

With a vicious jab, a golden-haired Fae woman pinned a writhing villager to a tree with her knife through his palm. His other palm she pinned to another tree before I could blink. Around her, five Fae stood laughing in a little ring.

"These white trees are birches," said one of the Fae. His beautiful fox-hair didn't disguise the cruel glint in his eye. He wore a bright chartreuse jacket sewn all over with red feathers. "I know a trick with birches. You pick two that are far apart and climb up to the high branches and tie a rope and then you pull the tree down as far as it will go. They bend more than you would guess. Then you pull the other one down, too. And you nail a mortal's feet to the branches. One to one tree, one to the other. And then you let both trees go."

Their laughter tinkled across my ears like a gentle breeze as horror froze my belly.

"That won't work," the golden-haired Fae said. The young man in front of her – Kenty Earthmover – moaned. My mouth went dry at the sound. It was the sound of someone past consciousness.

"I've seen it work," the fox-haired one said with a wink. He was holding something wrapped in cloth – a scythe, I thought. Had Kenty tried to fight with that? Or had he been caught out here unawares as he worked his fields?

"No, I mean, the nail will just pull out. Their flesh is too fragile. Better to lash him to the tree with leather. That won't break."

I felt like I might be sick, but I battled the feeling, drawing my arrow back.

"I wouldn't," Werex said, but I ignored him.

My first arrow hit the fox-haired Fae in the open neck of his jacket, the blood of his wound blooming around teeth tattoos and dripping to mingle with the red feathers. I began to nock a second arrow when the golden-haired female spun, her hands shooting up, ripples of something – magic? – dancing through the air.

I imagined her as small, small, small and in my cage.

She disappeared.

I turned to the next Fae, arrow aiming, but I was already too late. He was too close. I wouldn't be able to avoid him.

My heart was racing so fast I couldn't think clearly. I let the arrow go toward another Fae – one further away – at the same second that the close Fae crashed into me, knocking me to the forest floor and smashing his fist into my jaw.

I couldn't stop the cry of pain that shot through me. And then suddenly he moaned, and the pressure was off my chest. I rolled to the side and lurched to my feet. My cage had rolled away. My attacker had rolled with it. Where one of his eyes had been there was only a dark hole and his throat had been run through. Blood still spilled into the moss.

I gagged.

From the tree, Kenty moaned, but I was still looking for the third Fae that I knew should be there.

I found him on the ground, a sword being pulled from his chest.

No – not a sword!

A sewing needle.

Chapter Thirty-Four

"I'm sorry to say that your taste in companions is abhorrent, Nightmare," Scouvrel said, cleaning his sewing needle on the jacket of the dead man. "You make my skin crawl, you wicked thing."

"These men – " I began.

"Fae males and females."

"These men and women," I corrected sternly. I was more than my sex. So were they – evil or not. "Aren't my companions," I said, stumbling over to Kenty and whispering, "this is going to hurt," before pulling the blades from his hands.

He fell to the ground, clutching his hands to his chest. I leaned over him but Scouvrel called to me.

"Nightmare, listen to me."

I looked up. He was standing in a defensive position – low and aggressive as if he was planning to fight me. Which was crazy. Right?

"You should not be here," he said, eyes wild. "You should be running as fast and as far as you can run."

"None of us should be here," I said wryly. "And yet here we are. I need to stop my sister and I need to save my town."

"Oh, that you could do the impossible, Nightmare," he said, looking at me almost fondly. "Oh, that you could strike them to the core them as you have harrowed me. Oh, that we all could break the chains that bind us into roles we did not choose."

His shirt was open down to his navel despite the swirling snow and the frigid wind and I could see open gashes across his torso, bleeding into his smooth white shirt. His dark fitted coat hung to his knees and its ebony length was sewn with charcoal feathers, but even they were dark in places, and I knew only their dark color hid the blood wetting them.

I swallowed.

I was never sure if I should be terrified of Scouvrel or see him as a friend, if I should pity him, or disdain him. But he took these wounds for me. A sour taste filled my mouth at the sight of them, my eyes pricking sharply with unshed tears.

He was the worse for wear, his cheeks hollow and his dark locks tangled. The Balance had not been kind to him. That was my fault.

"I chose my role, unlike my marriage," I protested, though there wasn't much bite to my words. I turned back to Kenty, but he ignored me, a pained look filling his face as he rose, wavering to his feet and scampered off into the woods as fast as a winter hare. I watched him go. "No one chose for me. I'm no victim of circumstance or fate."

"You chose to be a sacrifice?" Scouvrel asked. He sounded so strange, like he was fighting some thought he didn't want to have. "To be your sister's chosen lamb for slaughter?"

"I chose to be a hunter," I said grimly, scooping up the cage from the ground.

And while my back was turned, I felt a shove. My face smashed into the tree and stars danced across my vision.

I blinked.

Twice.

I was in the cage.

The floor was slicked with blood and the only whole Fae still in it was Werex. I didn't want to think about what else was on the floor.

I gasped, scrambling to my feet and slipping on the bloody floor. My ankle twisted painfully.

Werex was fast. He slammed into me and I barely managed to dodge enough not to be crushed against the bars. The scent of burning flesh filled my nose as I rolled away.

Everything seemed to be happening at once.

My breath burned in my lungs as I panted, trying to suck in enough air to think.

My heart throbbed, beating faster, pushing me to action.

My hands tingled with the need to move.

My hands. There was something in one of them. I spared a lightning-fast glance at them. The bow.

Werex shot a small dart from something at his wrist. It struck my thick leather boot, embedding enough to bury shallowly in the leather.

Werex was charging again, axe slicing through the air. He was bigger than me. Faster than me. He had years of experience. I had no chance.

But I had to try.

My breath was coming too fast.

I dove for the ground, sliding over the slick, bloody surface, under his body, and then across to the other side of the bars. I hit them – hard – but used the momentum to twist so that I was lying on my back, bow arm up.

I yanked an arrow from my quiver, nocked it and loosed without aiming, hoping it would magically pierce his heart.

Werex bellowed, spinning to face me again, axe raised.

The arrow sliced through the air, spinning, curving unnaturally, and buried itself in his open, screaming mouth, angling upward. I gasped as he fell to the ground.

My heart hammered so loud that I couldn't hear anything else.

There was so much blood. I was used to blood, but not like this. Not with two yellow cat's eyes staring at me as if they might blink at a moment's notice.

I swallowed, my breath rasping out in gasps of agony.

Was this real? Had I just killed the Lord of Twilight?

Collecting my arrows with shaking hands, I paused to check my fallen foe. Yes. It was too real. The way he stared at me seemed to accuse me. I closed my eyes, but I still saw the stare.

I tried to scrub my bloody face with the back of my hand and clear my head enough to think.

The world spun around me, narrowing to this one moment, this thing I'd done. This fight that had almost killed me.

And then the realization hammered down on me. I was trapped. Again. Without any hope of stopping my sister.

I ran to the bars in a rage, stuck my head out and roared as long and hard as I could – right into the face of my captor.

He smirked at me.

"What have you done?" I asked, still shaking so hard that words were difficult to form.

"Exactly what I was ordered to do," Souvrel said with a cynical twist to his mouth. "If you didn't want the Balance ordering me around, then you shouldn't have sold me to him."

"But you threw me in a cage with the Lord of Twilight and he wanted me dead! I could have died. I almost did. And you just sat and watched."

"And see what a fine job you did of saving yourself? Perhaps all you needed was a little desperation and terror. I've heard that they can lend a person a fabulous level of concentration." He seemed utterly unconcerned.

"But I'm your wife!" I protested.

He smirked. "And a fine terrifying wife you are, soaked in the blood of the ruler of a Court. You'll have to teach me that little trick of yours with the arrow. I liked the irony of shooting him in his open mouth."

I shut my mouth with a click, staring at him for long moments.

"I could have died, and you don't care," I said flatly.

"You do yourself too little credit," he said coldly. "You were never going to die."

The cold wind blasted over us and I turned my back to it as tiny pellets of ice scored across my skin. Scouvrel seemed unaffected.

"Aren't you cold?" I demanded.

"I embrace the cold. It has all the charm of my wife's icy affections."

He'd betrayed me. I'd turned my back on him because I trusted him, and he'd betrayed that.

"I thought I could trust you," I said, my voice shaking.

He paused, staring at me. "I thought I was clear, Nightmare. I should not be trusted."

"I thought we were *married*," I said, still desperate to be proven wrong. Was this a trick? Was he really on my side despite how it looked? "I thought we were allies. I thought we were friends!"

"We are all those things." His glamor was painfully beautiful as he looked at me with such haunted eyes. "This, Nightmare, is how I treat my friends."

"I hate you," I said. "I hate you forever."

He smiled wickedly. "Good. You *should* hate me. You should despise me down to your very bones and triumph in my humiliation."

"Why would you say that?"

"Because I am bound to the truth and can speak no other."

Chapter Thirty-Five

There was no way to get rid of Werex's body unless I was going to be a monster like him. I refused to dismember him and throw his pieces through the bars. I was no monster.

But it was a miserable thing to have to stand on the far edge of the cage from him and to see what I'd done. He'd been alive. He'd been a thinking, feeling, living thing. And then I'd stolen all of that from him.

I tried not to think about how I was covered in his blood. I didn't want to panic.

Scouvrel lifted my cage so he could look at me as he slid through the clusters of Fae and the golems setting up camp around the village. Screams and laughter filled the air. I didn't dare look out of the cage. I couldn't bear to my friends being tortured for the amusement of the Faewald.

I couldn't stop my teeth from chattering, though. Hopefully, Scouvrel wouldn't notice. Hopefully, he wouldn't realize why.

I focused on his narrowed eyes as he looked across the gathered Fae, trying not to notice how many of them there were. I'd never seen a thousand people in one place before. I didn't like seeing so many now. It made me feel more vulnerable than I'd ever felt before, as if their sheer numbers surging into our world was some kind of violation.

"We have only minutes before I find my master and deliver you over to him," Scouvrel said in a low tone as he ducked around a group of Fae who were tying up captured soldiers to a large wheel they'd made of fresh-cut trees. I didn't want to know what the wheel was for. My imagination as already feeding me too many horrible ideas. This was what I'd been fighting against. And I'd lost. "If possible, I would like to gift you some information – as payment for the kiss I took earlier."

"What a bargain," I said dryly.

"I'd say so," he said with a smirk, as if he wasn't even noticing that a woman right beside us – Maebry Spinner, I thought – was shrieking like she was being killed as the Fae shoved her from one to another, demanding that she dance with them. "But we have no time for fond reminiscence of past crimes. You should know that the Balance plans to make you Fae – to make you immortal."

I shivered. I could feel his breath like a warm breeze gust over me as he leaned in very close. "Are you afraid, Nightmare? You should be. Be very afraid."

To my surprise, his expression was haunted as he spoke, shadowed with his own fears and etched deeply with lines of worry. He looked as if something inside was tearing him apart. I almost reached out to comfort him. Even the Fae deserved some compassion, didn't they? But no. Not Scouvrel. Not my betrayer.

"How do you become Fae?" I asked. "Do you have to ... kill someone?"

I glanced at Werex's dead body. I had already killed someone. Several someones. Guilt flopped in my belly like a fresh-caught fish.

"You become Fae by drowning in a river of blood." His expression was hard.

"You have to kill that many people?" I felt my eyes widening.

Why was I still surprised about any of this? I knew they were evil. I knew they loved horror and pain. So why did any of this surprise me?

At least I'd gotten the children out. That was the one good thing that I'd done.

"Oh, don't be so figurative, my Nightmare." Scouvrel's tone was almost affectionate. "I mean a real river of blood, of course. You will be literally drowned in it. Isn't that nice?" He bit those words off with a fury that belied his tight smile and made my stomach lurch. "You'll suck in the horrid death of someone else into your lungs until their desecration becomes a part of you and then you'll die. And we'll bring you back as a twisted nightmare like us. We call it 'The Glory' but only because 'The Horror' and 'The Repulsiveness' were already taken."

I gaped. "You've thought of things so horrible that they were already named 'The Horror' before you thought of *that*?"

"I keep telling you to run," he whispered, his eyes widening as if in pity. "I keep telling you to fear. You're a terribly foolish nightmare to keep coming back and haunting me despite it all. Do you think I take pleasure in your desecration?"

"Yes?"

He turned his burning eyes to me. "I had other plans for you, Nightmare. I still do."

"Then tell me what they are," I said through clenched teeth. "You've been bargaining and fighting to have me – to own me, to marry me – why? What is this bigger plan that dwarfs all the rest?"

"I wish I could tell you," he said, his eyes meeting mine. "Did you find your sister's apartments? Did you find what she wants?"

"She wants me dead so that she can rule the Court of Mortals."

"Yes. And what do you want?"

"I want a way to stop her from taking my people's homes and lives," I said.

He gave me a long dry look. "If you discovered what she wants, then you know that there is only one way to get that. You have to win her just like she is trying to win you."

"Scouvrel?" I asked, interrupting him.

He tilted his head to the side, listening.

"They stole you as a child and made you Fae. Does that mean that you also drowned in a river of blood?"

His glamor flickered for a moment, exposing his true nature. Feral eyes met mine and a hard expression filled his emaciated face. I gasped.

He shook his head violently, his face rippling through with masked fury and something that looked almost like fear.

His hand shook so hard that I had to focus on keeping my balance as the cage rocked side to side. My gaze was snatched away from his face and I realized we were walking into town – over a pile of corpses. The soldiers who had marched here with Sir Eckelmeyer.

My heart was in my throat.

"Don't try to distract me," he said between his teeth, his glamor returning. "The important part is that mortals may only be made immortal during the Feast of Ravens – when blood flows in rivers. This is their chance for The Glory. And you stole all the children they would have turned. Children collected over years of painstaking effort. The Balance thinks the only way to restore order is to drown you instead."

"And what do you think?" I asked a little breathlessly.

I was scanning for people I knew in the tumbled heaps along the streets. There was old Mayor Alebren, a kitchen knife in his hand. His head was a full pace away from his body.

My lips felt numb at the sight. I refused to look too long at the other fallen. I didn't want to see. I'd failed them all.

There was an angry roar from down the street – a mortal voice. A voice I knew.

"Leave them alone!" Olen. That was Olen.

As if all his small betrayals had never even happened, I felt my heart lurch to him. I wanted to defend him. I wanted to save him, too.

Scouvrel watched me with hooded eyes.

"Your strange capacity for forgiveness leaves me feeling hollow, Nightmare. What tortures mortals suffer on behalf of those who hurt them. What woes you will take on for one who did not earn the privilege. There's magic in that. A strange and wonderful mystery."

"Your point?" I asked through clenched teeth.

"That's what I want from you. It's what I've been fighting for from the moment you first put me in a cage," he whispered, holding the cage up so I could hear his words, see his eyes open wider, his lips tremble slightly as he confessed everything to me. "Absolution. Forgiveness. To be unwoven, untangled, undone."

I clutched the bars.

"How can I possibly give you all of that? I am no god. I am only mortal."

"With that magic. That magic of forgiveness that you possess."

"I don't see how," I whispered back.

He smiled, but this smile was not evil or twisted or wicked. It was pained and vulnerable.

"I do. And I will show you if we can live through this. But now, dearest Nightmare, you must dig deep and find a way to save your life, because my will is bound, and I cannot save you."

Chapter Thirty-Six

When we reached the town square, I couldn't help myself. I scanned the square for my parents. Had Sir Ecklemeyer found them? I pulled my blindfold up and down, scanning the real world and the spirit world, but I couldn't find a trace of them. I hoped they'd escaped and that I was the only one Sir Ecklemeyer was threatening. But hope was not enough. I wanted certainty.

The square was dominated by the Court of Twilight. Unlike the other Fae, they seemed less inclined to torture their captives and more inclined to set up a base of operations in the town. I caught a glimpse of Ghadrot leading a team of golems into town to clear away bodies and debris.

The Balance stood to one side, flamboyantly obvious even among the Fae with his half-dark, half-light appearance. There was a line of men bound by woven roots – because chains would burn the Fae. They'd been bound to a long rope. Olen was at the end of that line, a jagged wound running down his face and defeat in his eyes. The men, I realized, were his militia. Men and boys I'd grown up with. I felt a little shudder of fear at the sight of them all defeated, their homes sacked, their families either slaughtered or out there in the woods running.

How many innocents were still here when the Fae arrived? How many hadn't gone with my mother? The thought ached in my chest. I'd tried to tell them. I'd tried to warn them.

I hadn't done nearly enough.

And now, even if I saw my sister, I wouldn't be able to trap her. I had landed in my own trap.

With a burst of inspiration, I drew my sword. Maybe I could flee the cage with it. I slashed it through the air. Nothing happened.

Again.

Nothing.

It seemed that the cage negated the sword. Frustrated, I jammed it back in the scabbard. I'd need to try something else if I wanted out of this cage.

Scouvrel stepped over two bodies with wedding wreaths wound around their brows. Wedding wreaths I'd made. They were the bride and groom from the wedding a few weeks ago. Death had not parted them, after all.

I wasn't thinking right, I knew that. I should be crying. I should be shaking and retching and moaning. Instead, I felt hollow, as if the things I were seeing couldn't be real. As if I was watching someone else's life.

I swallowed.

Wreath. Writhe. Wraith. Wrath.

Scouvrel was right. They were all the same. The anger. The pain. The way it tangled and wove you until there was nothing left.

You're not thinking straight, Allie. You're giving up. And you can't give up. You can't surrender. I tried to find that flame within me again. It guttered in the winds tearing through my soul.

I slipped my blindfold down, watching Olen as his ends tangled up like a Fae.

A wrae.

A wreath.

I was going crazier by the moment. Did the insane know they were insane? Did my father know?

Soon they would open this cage and bring me out and make me Fae by drowning me in the blood of my friends. And what was I supposed to do about it? My only ally had to fight me against his will. My former friends and family were defeated.

I had no options.

Or did I?

I had the bow. But it was too small right now to harm anyone.

Hmmm.

And then my sister arrived.

She was glorious and beautiful, her winged hat like golden lace across her brow, the back of it kicking up like the tail of a turkey and woven in fine gold like the beams of a rising sun behind her head. She rode a white stag with ease as it seemed to flicker in and out of existence and at her side rode her lover, holding her hand in a show of unity – the Lord Cavariel.

"And so, the prodigal returns," she said lightly and around her, the Fae laughed.

The look of horror on Olen's face was priceless. He'd thought *I* was dangerous. He had no idea.

"I hear that you treated my family poorly while I was away, Olen Chanter," she said, letting her stag trot up to where he was tied. She reached out with a long sword and lifted his chin with the tip of it. "How shall I repay you for that?"

"I – I housed your family with my own," he stuttered. The Knight was gone and in its place was the boy from my girlhood. His shoulders were slumped in just the same way.

"And do you think that will save your neck?" she asked, her words a hiss.

"Oh, lay off him, Hulanna," I called, frustrated. "You're hardly one to judge. You had our father nailed to a tree for your pathetic blood sacrifices."

"What is this?" Hulanna asked, looking from Scouvrel to The Balance.

Scouvrel flinched.

"The Knave has just returned from fetching your sister, Lady," The Balance said, stepping away from where he was lounging to walk down the line of prisoners. He cuffed Olen casually in the jaw as he walked by and I flinched, only noticing that he was watching me after the fact. An eerie smile of satisfaction washed over his face. "She owes a debt to the Faewald."

My sister's eyes met his in a challenge. "She is a vital part of my plans. I need her to remain alive."

The Balance shrugged. "She is likely to be reborn as Fae. She has the tenacity for it."

Beside him, Olen hissed.

My sister frowned but she straightened so that she was even taller in the saddle, arching an eyebrow proudly. "If you are wrong about that, all this will have been for nothing. I have brought together most of the Faewald for the first time in all of known history to wage a common war. I will usher in a Golden Age. I will spill milk and honey over the Faewald and we will all dance with joy."

The Balance crossed his arms over his chest. "Be that as it may, Lady. My role is to see Balance and I will make it so."

She hissed. "Even over the common good? You would say this to your Queen?"

His eyebrows rose. "And so, the rumors are true."

I expected my sister to gloat, but I was surprised when a look of worry passed over her face. What did she have to be worried about?

Instead, Cavariel took a step forward, his charming smile growing even more beautiful as he increased the effect of his glamor.

"Come now, dear Balance," he said with a poisonous smile. "You did not think I married this mortal merely for her great beauty or for the heady enjoyment of her adoration."

"Didn't you?" The Balance lifted an eyebrow.

Cavariel laughed, "For long centuries the Faewald has been without a High King and Queen, but the addition of a new Court to our ranks and the conquest of the mortals shall reveal to all that we are the rightful High King and Queen of the Faewald. We are not demanding vows of fealty – yet – but we do hope that you will offer them willingly."

The Balance watched him for long seconds. "You know that in my role as The Balance, I may offer fealty to no one."

"Of course," Cavariel said graciously.

"But it would grant you favor in my eyes if you managed to quell the ravages to this town while I deal with this prisoner," he said nodding to me. "While your wife may prefer revenge, I would hate to have to restore balance here with the deaths of our own."

Cavariel nodded and Hulanna's face was peculiarly blank.

"Maim or injure all you like, but do not spill more lives on the ground," The Balance said, "Lest the Balance tip to the mortals and we four roles rise to defend them."

"As you say," Cavariel said, but the smile he regarded the prisoners with gave me chills.

"One moment," my sister said seeming to steel herself for something painful. "You are still here as witness, Balance. So, judge this, for with this sacrifice, I claim the Court of Mortals. I do not take without giving in return."

She stood – suddenly – in her stirrups on the back of the stag and lifted her two-handed sword. Her sword came down in a swipe so fast that it caught the light of the sun as it burst through the clouds, flashing so bright that I saw nothing but white for a moment.

There was a thump.

And then Cavariel's head rolled down the street and landed at Olen's trembling feet.

His body slumped to the ground.

I couldn't think. I couldn't breathe.

What had she just done?

"There will be no High King of the Faewald," Hulanna declared. "Only a High Queen."

"Your sacrifice is witnessed," the Balance said. "The life of your husband for your claim to the Court of Mortals. The Balance of power is maintained, and your conquest made binding by the claim of blood and sacrifice. So let it be recorded. So let it be proclaimed through the Faewald."

He nodded briskly and I finally remembered to gasp.

My sister's hard gaze met mine.

She'd just killed her own husband. She wouldn't hesitate to kill me. I didn't dare forget this. I didn't dare think that I could win her with compassion or pity. She was Fae to the core, evil to the core, grasping for power above all else.

"Come, Knave," The Balance said, "Bring our prisoner to the river of blood and let us drown her soul in murder."

Chapter Thirty-Seven

I tried to crane my neck to see what they were going to do to Olen and the others from my town. I tried to keep my eye on Hulanna, too. I felt dizzy – whether from trying to see with only one eye blindfolded or from what my sister had just done, or from what was about to happen to me, I couldn't have said.

I found the triumph in her eyes disturbing. She seemed less concerned over murdering her husband than I had been over defending myself from Werex. I tried to hold her gaze, but Scouvrel moved so quickly that my vision was obscured by his shoulders. He was holding me lower down now, as if I didn't matter to him.

"How far?" he asked The Balance.

"I saw a low dip in the ground just east of this town," The Balance said. "It was carved by the spring melt and rains." I knew the one he was speaking of. A little dip that filled with water up to my knees when the snow melted. Carter had a temporary bridge he pulled out of his shed and put over that dip in the Spring months. "It will be full enough by this time that we can enact The Glory there."

I fought against the fear that welled up inside me. I needed a plan. Scouvrel had told me that. He couldn't help me, but I could help myself. He'd also said that they had to take me out of the cage to do this.

So that would be step one. Get out of the cage. Would I have the chance to shoot before they took my bow and arrows? Did I have the heart to shoot Scouvrel?

I wasn't sure.

I could try a maiming shot, rather than a mortal one. But what if the arrow flew true with magic and took him in the heart? What if The Balance was too quick and took my bow from me?

I eased two arrows out of my quiver and nocked one, holding the other in my draw hand. I'd have to be fast. Faster than I'd ever been before.

I breathed deeply through my mouth, slow, controlled breaths. Fear and worry in, calm out. I focused on the bow in my hand and the feel of the arrow. And as I drew the stink of Werex in and the tormented screams of my people, I exhaled only calm, ever calm. I let the fire burn in my mind, burning up the fear and desperation, burning up the despair and turning it all into the fuel I needed to shoot two arrows quickly the moment I was free.

The Balance walked ahead of us with an awkward gait as if he preferred his wings and was irritated that he could not fly here. But no amount of awkwardness could keep us from eventually reaching the runnel of red blood flowing from Skundton.

The Balance stood in the blood, not concerned as it poured over his feet.

"We must act quickly. Soon, the deaths will end, and our opportunity will be over."

I shivered. If anything, ever, made me certain that the Fae were born of evil and nothing else, it was this right here.

"We are each born in blood and we die in blood for the blood is where the life is. Only in the blood of sacrifice can the old life be forgotten and the new embraced."

"Great. A lovely sentiment. Shall we add your blood to the mix?" I asked loudly, refusing to be anything but defiant in the face of this horror.

"Remove her from the cage, Knave, and mind my words. You will not let her escape or harm me. You will not let her kill herself by any means but this one. You will not prevent me from giving her The Glory or delay this in any way or in any way show her preference over me. If she threatens to harm me, you will overpower her and detain her. Is that understood?"

Scouvrel's lips were white as he nodded his head. His glamor had returned, but even now it flickered sometimes, showing me the emaciated, worn creature beneath it.

"Wait!" I called, shuffling my arrows to pull the frog out of my pocket. "First, take this."

I shoved my hand through the bar.

Scouvrel opened his palm and I dropped the frog into it. It became full-sized when it hit his palm and he jammed it into his pocket, his eyes going wide as they met mine. My blindfold slipped down the rest of the way. He nodded slightly as if acknowledging something, his lips pressed tightly together.

Did he recognize what it was? Did he realize what it meant?

"Enough delays," the Balance said. "Do not let her try to bribe you with trinkets. And do not offer her an easy way out," The Balance said. "Shake her out of the cage onto the ground with the body of Werex."

No! That was sure to make me lose my grip on the bow and arrows.

Think fast, Allie.

I scrambled to the side of the cage beside Werex so that he would fall out first. I didn't dare let go of the bow or the arrows. I tucked my chin just as Scouvrel opened the cage door and tipped it over. Werex slammed into the door. I slammed against him a moment later. He couldn't get through the gap.

Of course. I was the one who put him in the cage. Only I could take him out of it.

I positioned myself so I was standing on his back. Scouvrel shook the cage as The Balance cursed. Good. There was something I could still do to tangle their plans. I held onto my balance as he shook it, waiting, waiting, and when the moss floor was close, I leapt in the gap between Werex and the door, dropping to the mossy floor below.

I landed in the moss. I didn't have time to assess the situation. Not to note where my target was – nothing. I loosed the arrow.

I reached for a second, but the bow was snatched from my hand and tossed aside.

I looked up into Scouvrel's burning eyes. The arrow was stuck into his bicep. Not his heart.

Not his heart.

Even as his hands snatched my arrows away, I couldn't stop that thought from echoing through my mind.

The arrow was supposed to find and pierce an evil heart.

It hadn't pierced his.

My eyes were so wide that the air stung them.

He was shaking his head as if he was trying to deny what he was doing as he grabbed my arm and shoved it behind my back, forcing me to move as he wanted me to.

"Bring her here," the Balance said imperiously. "And give me her weapons. And yours. There will be no surprises today."

Scouvrel maneuvered me gently, but inexorably toward The Balance, seeming to be oblivious to the arrow in his arm despite the blood dripping from it. He handed over my bow and arrows, and his sewing needle rapier. Holding me in place with just one arm as I kicked and fought, he stripped me of my sword and scabbard, dropping them before The Balance.

The Balance smiled – a smile of ice and winter, of freezing to death without a fire.

"You thought to steal life from us. Now we steal life from you. Join us in immortality, in joined suffering, in painful subservience."

"I'm not afraid of you," I said through gritted teeth, fighting against Scouvrel. I should be terrified. I should be shaking and scared, but I wasn't.

I was furious.

I'd been betrayed. I was being backed into a corner. My best efforts had all failed and that didn't make me feel defeated or broken. It made me so angry. It made me so frustrated. I wanted to chew through leather. I wanted to rip down their tents and send them all running.

I landed an elbow strike to Scouvrel's ribs. His breath whooshed out, but his grip was only tighter.

"After this," The Balance said, you won't be able to lie like that. "After this, your mortal life will be over."

No.

I refused to accept that.

I wouldn't let me kill them. I would not be one of them.

"Take her to the edge of the flow," The Balance ordered. "Do not let her resist you."

Scouvrel forced me to frozen grass and wet snow, pushing me down to my knees. His lips quivered and his eyes were glassy, his glamor flickering on and off, but his arms were as strong as ever. Too strong for me to overpower. Blood dripped from his arm into the flow of blood in the ditch, but his arm never wavered.

He pushed my head down toward the water. Something hot hit my cheek. I twisted up to look at him. Was that a tear? Maybe this reminded him too much of his childhood. I twisted the emotional knife.

"You told me you were a betrayer, but I never thought I'd die by your hand," I said. "Add that to all the other reasons that you deserve the hell you live in."

"I've never claimed it was otherwise," he said tightly, but his eyes were drowning.

"I'll make you pay for this," I growled.

"Oh, how I long for that to be true, Nightmare. Oh, how I long for you to haunt me for all eternity."

I'd run out of options.

I was about to be drowned in blood.

"It's time," The Balance began.

And it was time. Time to take a last gamble.

"Push her – " The Balance began to order, but I interrupted him.

"Finmark Thorne," I whispered. "Forget all loyalties except those you have to me."

Scouvrel's eyes widened and his sudden inhale sucked the air out from between us. My gamble had paid off. I had his name.

" – into the blood and drown her!" The Balance was still talking. "Do this, as you have been ordered, Knave."

"Finmark Thorne. Let go of me and freeze for one minute," I whispered as The Balance spoke, my skin turning to goose-flesh at the gamble I was taking. Was it true? Could I order him to stop with his name?

Scouvrel's hands released me and he froze in place on his knees. His eyes were huge and brimming.

I didn't waste a second.

I ripped the arrow from his bicep and leapt toward The Balance.

The Balance's eyes widened as I crashed into his chest, his hands reflexively closing around my waist at the same moment that I plunged the arrow into his throat.

Chapter Thirty-Eight

The Balance gasped, clawing at his throat. His eyes seemed to flicker from one blue and one brown to both a bright cat's eye yellow.

"No!" Scouvrel whispered.

I drove the arrow deeper as the Balance choked. And then his hair faded from half white and half black to all black. And his wings disappeared.

He went limp under me and I clawed my way back up to my feet, gasping for breath. I felt strange. My head was spinning. It was hard to see properly.

I didn't feel like myself. I felt like I was someone else looking down at my own body.

The Balance had turned to a warbly version of himself – like how I saw mortals in my spirit vision. And then a white light shot out of his chest and up into the sky. Once it cleared the treetops, it burst – with a loud *bang* – into a thousand white stars. They formed a weigh scale for three heartbeats. And then they rained down on us.

In the distance I heard angry shouts.

"Nightmare," Scouvrel said carefully, rising to his feet, his eyes wide and hands spread open as if to show he was unarmed. "Nightmare, I bear you no ill will. Please do not kill me."

"Are you asking for a bargain?" I asked harshly. I didn't want to kill him. Not anymore. But his betrayal still stung to my core. Fury bubbled up into my heart.

His face was pale. "I'm asking you to spare my life."

"Then we are bargaining for your life," I said, scooping up my scabbard and buckling my sword belt in a single motion. The bow and arrows came next. I tossed Scouvrel his sword. The look on his face of fear and caution was unlike anything I'd ever seen from him before. I didn't stop to ponder it. I grabbed my cage from the mossy ground, shook Werex out of it – he landed right in the pooling stream of blood – and tied the cage to my belt.

"Yes," he said. "We are bargaining for my life and for my name."

I quirked an eyebrow at him. "It seems that you don't like being in my power."

His eyes grew dark as his pupils expanded so far that I could barely see the irises. "Trust me, Nightmare, I have enjoyed every moment of being in your power. Relinquishing my name will not lessen your hold over me."

I snorted. "Moments ago, you would have drowned me in blood."

"As I was bound to do. You will have a much fuller knowledge of the pain of that before you're ready for it."

"Oh?"

"Now that you're The Balance."

I gasped, my eyes darting to the corpse of the Fae who had once been The Balance. My heart began to pound in my skull.

"My old enemy," Scouvrel said. "The righter of wrongs. The destruction of good. The Leveler."

"No," I gasped. I couldn't seem to see properly. My vision was clouding over.

"That's what I said, if you recall. But you froze me. And there was nothing I could do to stop you."

"No." My eyes met his, wide and afraid, just like mine.

He crossed to me, stepping over the fallen body of the one whose role I had taken. He snatched my hands up in his.

"Nightmare. My most precious Nightmare." He licked his lips nervously, his eyes like those of a rabbit, darting this way and that. "In a moment, every Fae within miles will be here trying to kill you while you are vulnerable and before the mantle of your role asserts itself."

"But I'm not even Fae!" I protested.

"Nevertheless," he said, searching my eyes. "We ought to hurry. If you are willing to bargain for my life and name, then we must do that now. Trust me, Nightmare, every current of my soul follows you like the tide follows the moon."

"I don't know what tides or moons do," I said, pulling my hands from his. "But I do know that you lied to me, you betrayed me, and you tried to kill me."

"And now you command my whole being."

"Because I am The Balance?"

He shook his head. In the distance, I heard the crash of people and beasts hurrying through the forest.

"That tie broke with the old Balance's death. No, Nightmare. You have my name. And with it, you have me."

"Then I think I'll keep you," I said frostily. I drew my sword from my scabbard.

The trap was set, though I hadn't planned it. All I had to do was wait and hold my nerve. I shoved my bow into my quiver, grabbed the cage in my left hand and my sword in the right.

Steady, Allie. Steady.

I knew what I would do if I was a Fae and I saw that mark in the sky.

Which meant *I* knew what *she* would do.

"Then you will not kill me?" Scouvrel said warily.

"I own your life, but I find I like it where it is," I said, mimicking what he said about my braid. "But it is mine now. Do not cut it short. It is not yours to cut."

The glowing stag I'd been waiting for crashed through the trees before any other Fae made it to the little dip in the ground where we were hidden.

The moment I saw my sister's red hair streaming in the breeze, I smiled.

I remembered the look on her face right before she cut off her husband's head. I remembered her messy room, her dresses flung everywhere. I remembered the cruel glint in her eye when she looked at me.

And I thought of her as small.

And she was small.

So small, that now she was in the cage, stag and all.

I heard a shriek and a clatter from in the cage as the stag hit his antlers against the iron bars.

A roar of voices washed over us from the nearby bushes.

Scouvrel cursed, putting his back to mine as a ring of Fae surrounded us.

I slashed out with my sword, cutting the air before me and letting the cage fall to hang from my belt.

Hurry, Allie, Hurry!

I reached out, grabbed the tear, and forced it open, reaching back to grab Scouvrel by the collar of his coat and pull him through the tear in the world with me.

Excitement vibrated through me like a note through a mandolin string.

I had her at last.

At last.

Read more of Allie Hunter's story in Fae Pursuit: Book Four of the Twisted Fae series.

If you enjoyed Fae Nightmare, please consider leaving a review[1]. Reviews help fellow readers know what books to read and they help me know to prioritize my time and energy to that series. Thank you in advance!

---

1. https://www.amazon.com/review/create-review?asin=B07XLPZTFR

Behind the Scenes:

USA Today bestselling author, Sarah K. L. Wilson loves spinning a yarn and if it paints a magical new world, twists something old into something reborn, or makes your heart pound with excitement ... all the better! Sarah hails from the rocky Canadian Shield in Northern Ontario – learning patience and tenacity from the long months of icy cold – where she lives with her husband and two small boys. You might find her building fires in her woodstove and wishing she had a dragon handy to light them for her

Sarah would like to thank **Julie Thomas** and **Eugenia Kollia** for their incredible work in beta reading and proofreading this book. Without their big hearts and passion for stories, this book would not be the same.

Sarah has the deepest regard for the talent of her phenomenal artist Luciano Fleitas who created the gorgeous cover art that accompanies this book. Without his work, it would be so much harder to show off this story the way it deserves!

Thanks also to the Noble Order of Female Fantasy Authors who keep me sane – sort of. And for my beloved husband, Cale and sons Neville and Leif who are endlessly patient as I talk to them about bookish passions.

www.sarahklwilson.com[1]

Follow Sarah to keep up with fun updates:

INSTAGRAM[2]

---

1.   https://www.sarahklwilson.com/bridge-of-legends

[FACEBOOK](#)[3]
[AMAZON](#)[4]
[NEWSLETTER](#)[5]

2. https://www.instagram.com/sarahklwilson

3. http://www.facebook.com/sarahklwilson

4. https://www.amazon.com/-/e/B0064MSJRE

5. https://www.subscribepage.com/brandawareness